Richard L. Cary

Tales of the Turf

Richard L. Cary

Tales of the Turf

ISBN/EAN: 9783337344405

Printed in Europe, USA, Canada, Australia, Japan

Cover: Foto ©Andreas Hilbeck / pixelio.de

More available books at **www.hansebooks.com**

TALES OF THE TURF

AND

"RANK OUTSIDERS."

By Richard L. Cary, Jr.

("HYDER ALI")

WITH THIRTY-ONE ORIGINAL ILLUSTRATIONS
BY GEAN SMITH.

CHICAGO:
F. J. SCHULTE & COMPANY, Publishers,
298 Dearborn Street.

All the illustrations in this volume are from original paintings, made especially for this work, and are protected by the general copyright. The engraving was done by the Photo-Tint Company, Chicago.

PRESS OF HORACE O'DONOGHUE.

To the memory of

AUGUST BELMONT,

The typical racing man of America,

the accomplished patron of the Turf of the New World,

to whose noble example and enthusiastic patronage

its present status and prosperity

are mainly due,

this volume is appreciatively dedicated by

THE AUTHOR.

CONTENTS.

TALES OF THE TURF.

"RANK OUTSIDERS."

ILLUSTRATIONS.

· · · ·

INTRODUCTION.

THE writer deeply appreciates the privilege of writing the introduction to this charming collection of tributes to the glory of the turf.

To a man whose morning and noon-day of life have been spent in the love and labor of the turf these gems are indeed pleasant to hold and dwell upon. I have read but two turf poets — Adam Lindsey Gordon (the brilliant but ill-starred Australian) and Richard L. Cary, Jr., the author of this book. Here you may not find the tumultuous passages of Gordon, but you find a smooth and wholly enticing reiteration of the spirit of man's noblest sport. In these pages I have found the tender blended with the stern, the calm and beautiful tempering the rollicking and gay, the pathetic coloring the abandon, and the kind and the austere mingled in the seductive voice of song.

The glories of the turf; the almost divine enthusiasm that thrills all our veins in the sublime interest of contest; the wild excitement of the finish — all these are reëchoed in the flowing tones of a poet whose style is never labored and never stilted.

In the pages that follow many of my hours have been made pleasanter and better — they have given rise to a higher devotion to the superb animal whose admiration is with me, and with most of those who read these poems, a passion; and I commend them to all horsemen whose better moments are given to "the sweetness and the light" of this work-day world.

LESLIE E. MACLEOD,
Editor of The Horseman.

I.

TALES OF THE TURF.

TALES OF THE TURF.

. . .

WHY RAIN-IN-THE-FACE WAS SCRATCHED.

A ROMANCE OF WASHINGTON PARK.

Bob Jackson sat one night in June
And watched the roses red in bloom.
Beneath his straw hat, latest style,
Of Dunlap's make, there lurked a smile.
Dreaming he sat, and, where he dreamed,
The moonbeams through the casement streamed
Like a silver brook that had turned aside
In the dark, and sought a place to hide.

He dreamed of a rose-embowered cot,
By the trees half hid, on a corner lot,
By a turnpike road that stretched away
Among the blue-grass fields that lay
And smiled in the face of the summer sun,
Where the streamlets laugh as they onward run;
Of a slender form and a winsome face
That smiled in his with a fairy grace;
Of the home that he meant to have some day
When the wheel of fortune turned his way.

But when he glanced toward the far-off track,
Dark, with its stables over back,
His dreaming ceased, and he somehow thought
Of the three-year-old that day he'd bought,—

A likely colt, with a pedigree
That would almost reach from sea to sea,—
And he wondered how on earth he'd pay
The books all off if he lost next day;
For Bob had plunged in a plunger's way.

Bess Burroughs slowly climbed the stair,
Humming over an old-time air,
Such as mothers used to croon
In the old slave days by the dark lagoon,
To their pickaninnies, when the dark
Was only lit by the glow-worm's spark,
And the cotton-fields in their robes of white
Were tucked away by the goddess Night.

Over her shoulders, white and fair,
There streamed the wealth of her gold-brown hair,
While the dusky splendor of her eyes
Burned like twin stars in midnight skies,
And her dainty footsteps fell as light
On the marble stair as the feet of Night.
Blushing, she paused at the open door
Of the moonlit room, on the parlor floor,
To ask — you know 'tis a woman's way —
What horse he thought it were best to play
In the Drexel Stakes to be run next day.

Bob, smiling, rose, and with courtly grace
Escorted Bess to the vacant place
By the window seat, while the roses red
Bent low at the sight of her sunny head.
"Ah, Bess," he said, "in a racing way
I've not been right for many a day;
But this afternoon, when at the track,
I bought of Harper a handsome black,
By Ten Broeck, out of a War Dance mare,
The boys had christened Lord o' Clare.

"I like the way he moves; and, Bess,
I've backed him for a fortune!   Yes,
Unless he wins, my racing's o'er;
My colors will be seen no more.
But should he win, Oh, Bess! my dear,
Will you be mine this very year,
Before the roses fade and die
And flakes of snow across the sky
Are blown and fall to earth below?
Pray tell me, Bess,—I love you so!
For God's sake answer Yes or No!"

Bess Burroughs bent her gold-brown head;
Her cheeks were like the roses red;
Her dainty hand, a snowflake white,
Sought his, and, while a sudden light
Crept to her eyes, she whispered low:
"Bob, why will you keep plunging so?
Your Lord o' Clare can never win!
Papa's brown colt will beat him in.
If yours is first"— a look of pride
Shone in her eyes — "I'll be your bride
Before the roses fade and die,
Ere snowflakes drift across the sky.
To win, your Lord o' Clare must fly!"

And then she whispered low: "Good-night,"
And left him standing in the light
That through the open casement streamed,
And like a flood of silver gleamed
Upon the carpet, while she sought
Her dainty room and sat and thought,
All heedless of the flight of time,
Until the cuckoo clock chimed nine
Upon her mantel.   "Lord o' Clare

Must win!" she whispered.   Like a prayer
That sentence fell upon the air.

Jack Burroughs, withered, gray and bent,
Sat figuring, in calm content,
How much the Drexel, figured net,
Would yield the winner,—for he'd set

The Colored Archer.

His heart on winning that same race
With his brown colt, Rain-in-the-Face,
By Billet, out of Prairie Belle,
By Rebel, second dam Can't Tell,—
When Bess crept in with blushing face
For *his* opinion of the race.

"Why, Bess," the old man chuckling said,
"Rain-in-the-Face has got it dead!
There's not a horse that's entered there
Can make him run, save Lord o' Clare.

But even he can never beat
My gallant brown, who's strong and fleet
As any horse I've ever seen;
Yes, better, Bess, than Sweet Sixteen
Was at his age, and — well, you know
How fast that flying mare could go —
Aye! faster than the winds that blow!"

Bess bent and kissed the old gray head;
Then, blushing scarlet. softly said:
" Papa, I know Rain-in-the-Face
Can win, but in to-morrow's race
He must not start.   Please, for my sake.
Scratch the brown colt if you would make
Me very happy, and I'll bless
You all my life!"

               " Why, see here, Bess!"
The old man answered, while his eyes
Sought hers as if he would surprise
Her secret; " I have backed my colt,
And now you're asking me to bolt
The course, and all for Lord o' Clare.
It's both suspicious and unfair.
Old Harper can afford to lose
The stake.   No! Bess, I must refuse
To humor you.   'Twould be a sin!
Rain-in-the-Face must start and win!"

" No, papa, no!"   Bess softly cried;
" I know the colt's your pet and pride,
  But I want Lord o' Clare to win.
 Oh, papa, dear, I can't begin
To tell my reasons, but some day
You'll know them!   Let me have my way —
Please, just this once!" And eyelids wet
With tears were raised to his.

"My pet,"
The old man answered, "have your way;
The colt shall start some other day,
And Lord o' Clare shall win the race,
For I'll not start Rain-in-the-Face!"

Bess Burroughs, in a woman's way,
Thanked the old man and fled away
To her own room, and there, beside
Her snowy couch, she knelt and cried
For very joy, while down below
Bob Jackson, pacing to and fro,
Dreamed of a laughing, winsome face,
That, somehow, seemed to haunt the place;
Of dusky eyes, of hair gold-brown,
Until the lights were out in town;
Then sought his couch with whispered prayer
That He who ruled o'er earth and air
Would victory give to Lord o' Clare.

Next morn the hotel blackboard bore
Two lines not seen the night before:
"Rain-in-the-Face won't start to-day,
For women e'en must have their way!"
And much the turfmen marveled when
They read the words, for racing men
Knew old Jack Burroughs through and through,
And knew his winsome daughter, too;
But why he should not start the brown
Unless the colt had broken down
They could not yet quite understand.
How true it is that all the land
Is ruled and by a woman's hand!

Bob Jackson, rising ere the lark,
Between the daylight and the dark,

Had sought the track that lay asleep
Beneath the clouds, God's fleecy sheep,
To see himself that Lord o' Clare
Was given just the best of care;
Nor had he heard Rain-in-the-Face
Was not to start in that day's race
Until his trainer, chuckling low,
Said: "Burroughs' colt is not to go,
And, barring accidents, we'll win
The Drexel Stakes as sure as sin.
This time I'll lead the winner in."

Night slowly fled before the dawn;
The stars waxed dim and then were gone.
Across the fields a veil of gray
Came drifting where the moonbeams play;
Then Morning, rising from her bed,
Hurled at the Night her lance of red,
That, striking on the shield of Night,
Fell, broken, back in beams of light.
The rose-leaves quivered in the air,
The lark sent up its morning prayer,
And robins whistled everywhere;
The south wind whispered in the corn
That raised its spears to greet the morn;
And so a rare June day was born.
The day waned into afternoon;
The air was heavy with perfume;
A great crowd gathered at the course;
The gentler sex turned out in force.
The first two races had been run,
A rank outsider winning one,
The favorite in that same race
Not even running to a place;
And now the eager watchers wait
The Drexel Stakes!

Beside the gate
That led out on the level track,
There stood, a great crowd at his back,
The Californians' pride, Ben Bolt,
A slashing, handsome, big bay colt,
By Grinstead, out of Clara D.;
Full five years old he looked to be.
Beyond him, with a kingly air
And coat of jet, stood Lord o' Clare.
Sir Launcelot and Heart of Oak,
Romain, Falstaff and Artichoke
Made up the field, and in the sun
They looked like racers every one.

Beneath the club-house on the lawn,
Fair as a goddess of the dawn,
Bess Burroughs stood, her dusky eyes
Reflecting back the light that lies
Along the lovelit ways of June,
When earth and sky are both atune.
Beside her, leaning on his cane,
Jack Burroughs stood, and o'er again
Repeated: "Lord o' Clare will win!
Ben Bolt, I think, will chase him in.
Those Californy chaps don't know
That colt of Harper's. Down below,
At Louisville, I saw him run
A trial that humped the watches some—
He's fast as bullet from a gun."

A bugle blown upon the stand
Sent its wild notes across the land
To call the rival racers out,
And kerchiefs white were tossed about
When Ben Bolt slowly galloped by,
A silhouette against the sky.

Sir Launcelot and Heart of Oak,
Romain, Falstaff and Artichoke
Were greeted well.   A mighty shout
Caught Lord o' Clare when ridden out.

The colored Archer turned his head
And raised his cap of white and red;
While into old Jack Burroughs' eyes
There crept a look of great surprise.
He glanced at Bess and muttered low:
" Young folks must wed and old must go ! "
Then said aloud: " Well, I declare,
If Harper ain't sold Lord o' Clare,
And to Bob Jackson ! I can guess
Those reasons that you can't express.
I say, though, you're a sly one, Bess ! "

Bess Burroughs' cheeks were all aflame
A moment, then grew white again.
" Papa," she said, " I thought you knew
Bob loved me, and — I love him too !
If Lord o' Clare should win to-day,
He means to take your lass away,
If you will let him, ere the leaves
Turn red and gold, and while the sheaves
Still ripen in the autumn sun — "

" I thought you knew Bob loved me."

" Well, Bess, though you're the only one
That's left," the old man answered back,
" If you're disposed to bolt the track
With Bob, I will not say you nay,
For young blood must be served, they say;
It's been so since Creation's day."

Just at that moment, loud and clear,
A Californian standing near
Yelled :   " Who will bet against Ben Bolt ?
Five thousand that he beats that colt

Called Lord o' Clare!"   "I'll take you," cried
Old Jack, with true Kentucky pride,
And, putting up the cash, he turned
To Bess, with manner unconcerned,
And whispered in her blushing ear:
"They'll never beat him! Don't you fear!
Kentucky still can show the way
To Californy any day !
That cash will come in by and by
Most mighty handy.   Birds that fly
From old Jack's nest must needs fly high."

"They're off!"   The shout went up at last.
The pace, right from the start, was fast;
Ben Bolt and Lord o' Clare, abreast,
Were first away and led the rest;
Right at their withers, Heart of Oak
A head in front of Artichoke;
Romain and Falstaff, side by side,
Each swiftly measured stride for stride;
While, galloping behind the lot,
Came the iron gray, Sir Launcelot.

Around the lower turn they flew,
And then Romain's red, white and blue
Was first to show, with Artichoke
In second place; next Heart of Oak,
While Californy and Kaintuck
Ran head and head back in the ruck;
Right next to them, Sir Launcelot,
With Falstaff "tailing" off the lot.
The dust that rose, a golden cloud,
Half hid them from the eager crowd.
The silks and satins, gleaming bright,
Were ever shifting in the light —
A flock of humming-birds in flight.

Into the stable-turn Romain
Still showed the way, and then again
Another change, and Heart of Oak
Sailed to the front with Artichoke.
Sir Launcelot flew like a bird
Around the bend, and soon was third.
A shout went up: "Just see Ben Bolt!
And like a flash the Grinstead colt
Shot out in front! Cheers rent the air.
Right on his flanks hung Lord o' Clare,
While, only half a length away,
With steady strides there came the gray.
A furlong out whips flashed in air.
"Ben Bolt is beaten!" "Lord o' Clare
Will win!" Bess Burroughs breathed a prayer.

On toward the goal the racers swept,
And, inch by inch, the black colt crept
Up on the leader, while the gray
Was still but half a length away.
A distance out Sir Launcelot
Came on the outside, like a shot,
And then joined issue with the pair.
Here Murphy called on Lord o' Clare,
And, putting forth his giant strength,
The black colt won by half a length.
Sir Launcelot, fleet as the wind,
Left Ben Bolt half a head behind.
Bess Burroughs waved her 'kerchief white,
Her dusky eyes with love alight —
And wore a diamond ring that night.

.   ,

Within a rose-embowered cot,
Half hid by trees, on a corner lot,

A level turnpike road beside,
Bob Jackson and his bonny bride
Are living now; while on the gate,
In summer, when the day grows late,
A laughing, bright-eyed urchin swings
And prattles of the sport of kings
To old Jack Burroughs, standing near;
And from the cottage, low but clear,
Comes floating on the summer air
The song that once upon the stair
Bess Burroughs hummed in days gone by.
" Ah me, how quick the summers fly ! "
The old man, glancing o'er the place,
Says, thinking of Bess' happy face;
" I'm glad I scratched Rain-in-the-Face ! "

HOW SMUGGLER BEAT THE MAID

A TALE OF THE CENTENNIAL YEAR.

I.

Draw back the curtains, Father Time, and pin them fast with
     spears;
  Call out the flyers, dead and gone, of fifteen years ago—
The heralds of a flying age, that even now appears,
  Swift climbing o'er the mountain peaks, white with their caps
     of snow.
What though the sulky-wheels be stilled, a driver gone to sleep
Beneath a little mound of sod, where tangled grasses creep?
So long as in the breast of man an honest heart shall beat,
And kings and queens of equine birth in battle royal meet,
Will Mem'ry journey backward to that golden summer's day
That gave to one a kingly crown and took a crown away.

Let's trot it o'er,—that greatest race the century has seen,—
For never grander field has trod a trotting-track. I ween,
Than took the track at Cleveland, where a king dethroned a
  queen.

II.

The sun that ushered in the day looked down upon the corn,
  That raised a hundred thousand spears all flashing in the
    light,
To greet a queen that jogged the track in pride at early morn,
  Then faced about to greet a king that strode the track at
    night;
For from the far-off Kansas plains, where rippling grasses grow,
And ox-eyed daisies star the sod like flakes of living snow,
Had come a slashing big bay horse, with flashing hazel eyes
That held imprisoned 'neath their lids the light of sunset skies;
And boldly thrown a gauntlet down and dared a queen to meet,
While fawning courtiers knelt around, astonished, at her feet.
But Doble picked the gauntlet up and swore a lance he'd break
With Charley Marvin then and there, just for his lady's sake.
Then Dan Mace said he'd take a hand, and so did Charley
    Green,
While Johnston, armed all cap-a-pie, appeared upon the scene.
Ah! one there is, gone fast asleep —God keep his mem'ry green.

III.

Beneath the grand stand met that day the men from ev'ry State;
  From North and South, from East and West the trotting cohorts
    came.
They argued things from every point and figured out the slate;
  Then, looking o'er the records, said, " She'll get there just the
    same ! "
For Goldsmith Maid, the trotting queen, was then just in her
    prime;
Her record, " Two-fourteen," still stood unchallenged by old Time.

She skipped along with airy grace and ruled a queen by rights
Of conquests made on many tracks o'er ladies fair and knights.
"And who," they asked, "is this who comes from out 'the wooly
          West,'
To beard the tigress in her den, the eagle in her nest?"
"'Tis Smuggler," Marvin answered back, "and we shall wrest
          the crown
From Doble's little trotting queen before the sun goes down."
Then Mace he swore a mighty oath that Goldsmith Maid should
          win,
And Green with Lucille Golddust vowed he'd help Budd Doble in,
While Peter Johnston winked his eye and wicked looked as sin.

IV.

The ladies in their fleecy robes gave back Dame Nature's smiles.
    Their bright eyes gleamed more brightly than the jewels that
          they wore.
Fond cavaliers above them bent, lured by their graceful wiles;
    While music of the laughing waves came faint from Erie's shore.
A thousand dainty fans of lace were flutt'ring in the air,
As though a swarm of butterflies had come to hover there;
A thousand dainty handkerchiefs tossed on the south wind's
          breast—
'Twas like a cloud of snowflakes blown across a flowery heath.
Eyes spoke to eyes that spoke again, and laughter low and sweet
Went rippling o'er the crowded stand—a zephyr in the wheat.
Bon-bons were wagered everywhere, and gloves a thousand score
Would find new owners ere the night came down upon the shore.
A statue grand upon the stand stood Smuggler's owner there;
A statuette was Doble's wife, upon her lips a prayer.
Around the pool-stands surged the crowd in rough but noisy glee,
While wagers flew about like hail and words were bandied free.
'Twas Goldsmith Maid against the field, at any odds, you see.

"She beats him home by half a length. The courtiers smile again."

v.

Loud clangs the bell that calls them out, and, 'midst a storm of
    cheers,
Budd Doble jogs the trotting queen up slowly by the stand;
Judge Fullerton, prince of the realm, with Dan Mace next
    appears —
The Wizard of the Sulky bowing low on every hand;
Now Lucille Golddust comes along, her driver Charley Green,
And P. V. Johnston follows fast, he piloting Bodine.
The storm of cheers, that died away like thunder in the sky,
Bursts out again as Marvin jogs the mighty Smuggler by.
Pretender though the horse may be, pretender to a throne,
Where Goldsmith Maid has reigned a queen for many years
    alone,
He hath a royal bearing, and his flashing hazel eyes
Reflect the lightning's glint that plays along the western skies.
They wheel beyond the judges' stand; they're marshaled for the
    fray.
Each man's a master of the craft that holds the reins to-day.
Let drums be stilled and bugles mute, while heralds clear the
    way !

vi.

Two false attempts, then down they come, but Smuggler lurks
    behind;
The others level reach the wire, and " Go," the starter cries;
They sweep around the lower turn as swiftly as the wind;
Each stride they take is measured by ten thousand pairs of
    eyes.
Judge Fullerton has left his feet ! The Maid is out in front;
Determined as was Joan of Arc, she bears the battle's brunt !
Bodine is in the second place ! With muscles made of steel,
The mighty Smuggler strides along — he's at the gelding's wheel.
Resistless as the torrent's rush in mountainous ravine,
He sweeps into the second place, a heaven-made machine.

The noisy crowd is hushed and still.   He's gaining on the Maid,
And now they swing into the stretch. " Come on ! Come on, you
     jade ! "
The stallion falters.   What was that ?   A shoe that's cast in air;
The answer to a muttered wish, a woman's whispered prayer.
He comes a cyclone through the stretch, born on a Kansas plain.
She beats him home by half a length.   The courtiers smile again.
That rush electric fired the blood like lightning's tongues of flame.

VII.

With one false start, they're off again.   Like arrow from a bow
    The trotting queen shoots to the front, and Smuggler leaves
        his feet.
Her sulky like a storm-tossed bark is rocking to and fro;
    She's shod like Mercury of old —'twas wings that made him fleet.
The stallion's settled down at last -- great Scott ! a distance out.
With only dust that's backward blown to show to him the route.
He hears the noise of iron-shod hoofs that echo from the track,
The humming of the flying wheels, the noisy whips that crack.
He borrows swift Pegasus' wings,—they're lent him from the
        skies,—
And, like a blood-hound on the trail, around the circle flies.
The Maid, a victor, reached the wire.   Down drops a blood-
        red rag.
Thank God for that wild burst of speed that beat the distance flag.
For Smuggler's just ten lengths away, his breast bedecked
        with foam;
He looks a giant cast in bronze, and left to trot alone,
For Lucille Golddust and the rest, all, all have beat him home.

VIII.

With two heats to her credit now, the Maid is sure to win;
    You'd bet a brownstone front she would against a peanut-stand.
Through overconfidence in Eve was Adam made to sin,
    And Providence has oft o'erturned the best schemes ever
        planned.

Again the Maid shoots to the front and speeds around the turn.
Her hoofs, that twinkle through the dust, you scarcely can discern.
Judge Fullerton is two lengths back, with Lucille at his wheel;
The Kansas stallion coming next, while Bodine foots the reel.
Lucille has taken second place before the half is passed,
While 'way on the extreme outside comes Smuggler, trotting fast.
He leaves Judge Fullerton behind! he bids Lucille good-by!
He scarcely seems to touch the earth, but rather seems to fly.
He comes a demon in the stretch; he's at the leader's girth.
The queen's attendants silent are.   They've lost their looks of
    mirth.
'Tis vain that Doble plies the whip and lifts the mare along;
That cyclone from the Kansas plains is coming mighty strong.
"God save the queen," the courtiers cry, but all in vain the
    prayer —
He beats her by a head and neck, while hats are tossed in air.
Pretender, eh? and to a throne?   Ah, Doble, have a care!

IX.

They're off again at second trial, with Smuggler two lengths back.
    The queen goes sailing off in front, Lucille at Smuggler's
        girth,
While Fullerton is lapped outside, and Doble, looking back,
    Has reason good to think he holds a mortgage on the earth,
For never yet in patent trap was rat more surely caught
Than was the stallion pocketed — so everybody thought.
Three of the greatest drivers that the trotting-track has seen,
Three of the fastest horses — aye, and one of them a queen —
Have formed a combination that shall make her throne secure.
"They've got him fast!" the watchers cry; "the Maid will win
    it sure!"
They hold him till the stretch is reached — they'll never let him
    through.
Great Scott! what's Marvin thinking of?   Good Lord! what can
    he do?

He sudden takes the stallion back, then brings him on outside.
The same cyclonic rush again, the same resistless stride.
Green sees the white face rushing by and quickly turns about,
Then loudly shouts above the din, " Look out there, Budd; he's
　　　out ! "
And Doble, rattled, seeks the whip and lays it on the mare;
He fairly drives her off her feet and up into the air.
True as a bullet to its mark the stallion rushes by.
Again he beats her by a neck, while hats are tossed on high,
And cheers like rockets rise from earth and break against the
　　　sky.

X.

The courtiers wear a troubled look; there's danger in the air;
　　The throne is trembling at its base; a rival's drawing nigh.
" God save the queen ! " again they shout,—'tis like a frenzied
　　　prayer,—
　　And hope that Night her starry scarf will fling across the sky.
Six times they score, and then they're off.　Good Lord, another
　　　game !
'Tis Fullerton that shows the way; 'tis Mace's fertile brain
That's planned the scheme by which they hope to bolster up the
　　　throne
On which the queen has sat for years and ruled her hosts alone.
The Maid is trailing in the rear; she hangs on Smuggler's wheel.
You catch the flash of silvered rims while sulkies rock and reel.
The trick is old as are the hills; naught 's new beneath the sun;
For every jock has played the game—they call it " two pluck one."
The leader's flying like the wind—he's struck a storm-cloud's
　　　gait;
He's carried Smuggler to the half; the watches mark "one-eight!"
His mission's finished on the turn, and now the Maid goes out
To catch the steed they hope to tire by forcing him the route.
'Tis all in vain.　The stallion comes along in conscious pride;
There is no soft part in his heart, no falt'ring in his stride.

"The queen is dead.   Long live the king!"   Get ready now to
  cheer;
Let drums be beaten, bugles blown, to greet the victor here !
Resistless as the whirlwind's rush where summer winds have
  played,
He finishes the race alone, just as the sunbeams fade
Into the night; and that is how bold Smuggler beat the Maid.

Let fall the curtains, Father Time; call all the phantoms back
You brought from out the misty past to trot a race to-day.
Their ghostly hoofs no echoes wake when pounding on the track;
The driver's lips that Death has sealed can neither scoff nor pray.
The king that won, the queen that lost, both, both have passed
  away.
Dan Mace has driven out of life.   Above his dust to-night
The snow lies like a fleecy scarf and hides the mound from sight.
The frost is thick in Marvin's hair, while Doble looks alone
Of that quintette as young as when the queen was overthrown.
Though fifteen times the flowers have bloomed and fifteen times
  the snow
Has fallen to the breast of earth and drifted to and fro,
Since Smuggler won a kingly crown, the mem'ry of that scene
Will live as long as roses blush, as long as grass grows green.
Now Marvin brings, from Golden Gates, Sunol, the new-crowned
  queen.

IKE MURPHY'S RIDE.

(Monmouth Park.)

Listen, my children, and you shall hear
Of Murphy's ride, and I'll make it clear:
On the tenth day of August, in eighty-five —
Many a man is now alive
Who remembers that famous day and year —

He said to his boss: "If McLaughlin rides,
   As I think he will, in this great race,
My spurs I'll not touch to the gelding's sides,
   But I'll let him go out and make the pace;
He may make it fast or make it slow,
But I'll lay behind and I'll lay quite low,
Ready to ride when the finish comes,
Though the wind may whistle and blow great guns,
While the Dwyers curse and the bay horse runs."

Then he said, " I'll win!" and he crossed the track,
Never once stopping or looking back,
Just as the sun from behind a cloud
Looked down at earth and the howling crowd
Of bookmakers that stood at bay,
And wondered which it was best to play,
As their fickle memories magnified
The races they'd seen McLaughlin ride.

Meanwhile his boss through the howling crowd
   Wonders and listens with eager ears,
   Till in the sunlight around him he hears:
" I'll lay on Miss Woodford five to four,"
The roar of voices that shouted it loud,
   And the low, sweet voice of the " pencileers "
As they booked his bets and cried for more.

Then he climbed to the top of the big grand stand
By the wooden stairs, with a heavy tread,
To the private boxes overhead,
And startled the ladies from their seats
On the painted benches that round him lay,
Brown with dust in the yellow day,
By a winding staircase, somewhat tall,
To the highest place there was of all.

Where he stopped to listen and look down
A moment on the girls from the town,
And the sunlight gleaming over all.

  .   .   .   .   .

Meanwhile, impatient to start and ride,
With jacket of green and cap beside,
  On the opposite side Ike Murphy stood.
Now he patted bold Freeland's neck,
  Now looked away to the distant wood,
While the noble racer stamped the earth,
Then turned to bite at his saddle-girth;
But mostly he watched with eager eyes
The rival jock and the starter's flag
That hung o'er the white fence standing near,

Like a blood-red rag in the sunlight clear.
But, lo! as he looks on the grass, it falls,
A glimmer and then a gleam of red;
Then he tightens the bridle and turns around,
And smiles, with a nod, as he softly calls
To his noble horse that spurns the ground.
A hurry of hoofs in a wild, mad dash —
Two steeds in the sunlight, two shapes in the day,
And beneath them the pebbles struck out from the clay
By two thoroughbreds flying and under the lash.
That was all, and yet through the dust, you may say,
The fate of an owner was riding that day.
That night there was many a ticket to pay,
When the tale was told by the lightning's flash.

               .

You know the rest. In the books you have read
How McLaughlin kept the brown mare ahead,
Till Freeland came with a sudden dart
At the finish, and Isaac proved too smart

For the Dwyers' jock; how at the last
He nailed him just as the post was passed.
Oh, I tell you it was a close-run race,
And it gave to Murphy the pride of place.

WHEN HUNTRESS WON THE STAKE.

(WASHINGTON PARK, CHICAGO, 1889.)

I.

It was an ideal racing-day: the sun was swinging high,
A dazzling golden globe of light beneath an azure sky;
The roses, blushing red and white, were climbing o'er the wall,
While robins in the leafy wood were sending back the call
Of meadow larks that upward sprang from out the tangled
    grass,
To whisper to the fleecy clouds that swiftly'd come and pass.
It was a peaceful summer scene, but echoes soon would wake
The drowsy cattle from their sleep if Huntress won the stake.

II.

The grand stand held a brilliant crowd.   In fashion's bright array
The ladies had turned out in force to see the race that day.
The club-house steps, with members thronged all through those
    golden hours,
Seemed some pagoda fringed with black and bursting out with
    flowers.
The hum of myriad voices seemed to echo through the stand —
'Twas like the moaning of the sea that's heard upon the sand,
Though now and then some eager voice the humming sound
    would break,
The while it asked, "Will old Montrose or Huntress win the
    stake?"

III.

The betting ring was thronged with men —the smooth asphal-
tum floor
Gave back in echoes loud and long the ring's deep, sullen roar.
About the bookies' box-like stands the crowd surged like a sea;
'Twas "six to five" and take your pick — no choice there seemed
to be;
And ten to one 'gainst Robin Hood, but no one but a flat
Who didn't know a horse from mule would nibble e'en at that.

"'You've got him, Jim!' 'The mare will win!'"

A duel to the death 'twould be, and many hearts would ache
Unless the gallant Hankins' mare should carry off the stake.

IV.

A bugle sounding loud and clear was echoed by a shout,
While through the open paddock gate McLaughlin, riding out
Upon the famous chestnut mare, was greeted with such cheers
(I seem to hear their echoes now come floating down the years)

As greeted him but once before upon a Western track,
When, winner of the great Eclipse, he rode Miss Woodford back
To weigh in at St. Louis. Ah, many a man he'd break
If Huntress, Springbok's daughter, failed that day to win the
    stake.

V.

Then old Montrose, with Lewis up, swept by with steady stride,
With arching neck, with flashing eyes and nostrils opened wide.
Again the cheers swept o'er the track and hats were tossed in air,
For never Western course had seen a grander-looking pair.
Robin Hood passed all unnoticed, with Winchell on his back —
What chance had he in such a race, when run on such a track?
They stand together at the post; a pretty scene they make;
The flag falls — now will old Montrose or Huntress win the
    stake?

VI.

The purple with canary sash goes dashing by the stand;
He's leading Huntress by a length; McLaughlin has in hand
The chestnut mare that carries well the black with orange sash.
While Robin Hood, already last, don't figure in the dash.
Around the lower turn they sweep beneath the blazing sun;
And still the Labold colors lead — the race is now half run.
"Montrose will win!" the shouts go up, and all the echoes wake;
"Five thousand to three thousand now that Huntress wins the
    stake!"

VII.

Bold Robin Hood was done for ere they reached the upper turn.
It took a royal field glass then the leader to discern;
But those who watched them closely saw by the sunlight's flash
That gaining, surely gaining, was the black with orange sash.
A furlong out Montrose still led; there fell an awful hush
Upon the multitude. It seemed as though one felt the rush
Of storm-clouds through the sultry air, that would in thunder
    break,
If Huntress in that dash for cash should carry off the stake.

VIII.

A sixteenth more, the race was o'er — one-sixteenth of a mile;
'Twas scarce the beating of a heart, the flitting of a smile;
'Twas scarce the ticking of a clock, a pendulum that swung,
The rattling of those flying hoofs that echoes wake among
The shadows underneath the stand. "Come on there, old
    Montrose!"
"You've got him, Jim!" "The mare will win!" The tumult
    louder grows.
The race is run, the mare has won, and cheers the echoes wake,
For Huntress, Hankins' chestnut mare, has carried off the stake.

.   .   .   .   .   .

Above the winner of that race the grass is growing green,
For Death with icy fingers stopped and touched the Western
    queen.
Let's hope that in another world, if other world there be,
She roams among the clover from the touch of halter free;
That, when some time in after years this racing tale is told,
And, standing by life's sundown bars, we dream of days of old,
'Twill stir again our sluggish blood, and bid fond memories wake,
To look back to that summer day when Huntress won the stake.

DANDY JIM'S DREAM;

OR, HOW THE BROWN COLT WON THE DERBY.

In a little, low, thatched stable, in the Crescent City, lay
"Dandy Jim," a light-weight jockey, fast asleep upon the hay,
While the rain-drops, softly falling on the roof, sang merry
    rhymes;
And the night wind on its bosom brought the sound of
    Christmas chimes.

O'er his couch Death's angel hovered, with his dark and
    outstretched wing,
Like a messenger awaiting the dread summons from his king;

But the jockey's careworn features wore a sunny, peaceful smile —
Jim was dreaming of the horses, and his old home by the stile.

All the old life passed before him as he lay there, fast asleep;
Childish prayers he softly murmured, praying God his soul to
    keep;
While the gray-haired, wrinkled trainer, in whose eyes the tears
    would come,
Muttered softly, "Jim is dying!   Angels bring him dreams of
    home."

Slow from Time's hands dropped the minutes, as the long night
    drifted by;
Then there came a touch of crimson in the far-off eastern sky,
And the dying jockey, waking, called the trainer to his bed.
"I've been dreaming, John," he whispered; "listen what my
    dreamings said:

    " I thought that I lay awake in the grass,
        In the sunshine warm and bright,
    Where the birds and the shadows come and pass,
        And the cat-birds call at night;
    And the big brown colt in the stable there
        Was roaming about at will.
    There wasn't a sound in the summer air,
        Save the busy water-mill —

    " Save the noise of the brook that laughed and sang
        'Midst the rushes cool and green,
    And a robin's song in the wood that rang —
        Oh! 'twas a peaceful scene.
    I could see the old farm-house, where it stood
        Just under a maple tree;
    I could catch a glimpse of the distant wood,
        The sheen of the far-off sea.

"At the end of a mile a gray colt led; the black at his withers lay."

" I could see the apple trees, white with bloom,
  That stood by the em'rald lane,
And the roses nodding to welcome June,
  The touch of her hands again.
My mother I heard, as she softly sang
  The ballad I used to know,
Of the flower that up from the ashes sprang
  With its petals white as snow.

" Then I thought, somehow, that I fell asleep;
  I dreamed of the old race-track,
With the grass in the paddock ankle-deep,
  And the stables over back;
And I heard the sound of the noisy crowd
  One hears on a Derby Day;
And the bookies' shouts as they cried aloud
  The odds that they wished to lay.

" And I saw the brown colt galloping by:
  He went to the starting-post
With a nervous fire in his flashing eye;
  In the saddle rode a ghost.
The jockey men saw was a stranger there,
  But the ghost that rode was me,
With the grave-yard dust in my tangled hair;
  And the colt moved strong and free.

" Then I saw the starter's flag go down,
  And 'They're off,' I heard them cry.
A black was ahead of your slashing brown,
  And a chestnut colt close by.
At the end of a mile a gray colt led;
  The black at his withers lay;
While at his saddle-girths the chestnut sped;
  The brown was a length away.

" Then a cry went up from the betting-stand,
  'See ! the big gray colt is done !'
'Ha ! the chestnut wins; he is well in hand.
  Great God ! See the brown colt come !'
Then the brown and the chestnut, side by side,
  Drew out from the black and gray;
For a moment they raced on stride for stride,
  Then the brown colt drew away.

"Coming on like an arrow, strong and true,
  We won by a length or more;
He had carried away the ribbon of blue,
  And I heard the great crowd roar.
But the jock men saw was a stranger there,
  While the ghost that rode was me.
Then I shook the dust from my tangled hair,
  But never a man could see.

" I want you to make me a promise, John,
  That you'll start that colt for me
In the Derby, and I — I'll ride him, John,
  Though my ghost you may not see."
This the trainer promised, then turned away
  As Jim's lips moved in prayer.
And his spirit fled in the dawning gray,
  And left but a casket there.

.   .   .   .   .

In a little, low, thatched stable, in the Crescent City, lay
Dandy Jim, the light-weight jockey, dead upon his couch of hay.
Death the gift the Christ-child brought him, as he changed the
    cross to crown,
When he called the lad, grown weary — bade him lay his burdens.
    down.

Slowly drifted by the winter, and the spring came on apace.
One by one the books were opened on the great blue-ribbon
race.
'Gainst the chestnut, " ten to seven " was the odds, and lower down
On the list, and marked at forties, was John's slashing colt, the
brown.

Looked he every inch a race-horse, but, when moving in his
work,
He would somehow try to bolt it, and he acted like a shirk.
Still John piled the money on him, and once to a friend he said:
" My brown colt will win the Derby ! 'Tis a promise from the
dead."

Derby Day at last arriving, he was galloped by the stand,
With a stranger in the saddle; but he answered each command,
Like he felt some hidden pressure on the slender bridle-rein —
Felt the light touch of a master; yet he knew not whence it came.

Fell the flag, as Jim had dreamed it, with the black colt in advance;
Then the brown, and then the chestnut closely followed in the
dance.
At the mile a gray was leading, while the black beside him lay;
At his saddle-girths the chestnut, and the brown a length away.

" 'Tis Jim's dream," the trainer muttered, as they straightened
out for home.
" Now the chestnut colt is leading. Great God ! see the brown
colt come!
Drawing level with the chestnut, puts he forth his giant strength;
Has him done for at the distance; wins by just an open length."
.　　.　　.　　.　　.　　.　　.

By a little, low, thatched stable, on a famous racing-track,
Stood the winner of the Derby, with a great crowd at his back,
While the trainer told the story of his dying jockey's dream:
" 'Twas his spirit, men, that rode him ; 'twas his ghost no man
hath seen."

AN OWNER'S OPINION.

Eh?   What do I think o' my hoss's chance?
  She hasn't the ghost o' a chance at all.
Reckon when others are leadin' the dance
  You'll find her down at the foot o' the hall.
She ain't bin out o' the stall fer a week,
  Ain't no account, and she never will be.
So you've backed her, eh?   Well, you hear me speak;
  She never will be in the hunt.   Now see!

A pretty good mare she was in the fall,
  Speedy an' game, an' could carry her weight;
Galloped at Nashville away from 'em all—
  Beat some o' the best they had in the State;
But she got lung fever an' nearly died;
  She's a little thick, right now, in her wind;
She's sulky, too, an', whenever she's tried,
  Seems ter delight in bein' behind.

What was there agin her?   Twenty to one?
  There ought to be fifty, upon my word.
Why, after the manner in which she's run,
  The layin' o' short odds like that 's absurd.
That 's her, sir, gallopin' now up the track.
  Eh? Looks pretty well, did I hear you say?
That fellow o'er yonder, sir, is the crack,
  An' he is the colt that should win to-day.

Eh?   What will I take for the old brown mare?
  Wall, she ain't for sale, I'm sorry to say,
As she may round to with the proper care
  An' win me a thunderin' stake some day.
No, she isn't handsome, that I'll allow;
  Neither am I, so we make a good pair.
But I haven't quite lost faith yet, I vow,
  In the racin' powers o' my old brown mare.

No, she hasn't a chance on earth to-day
  To win, or even to run to a place,
An' you're mighty foolish, I think, to play
  A hoss like her in this sort of a race.
I jest put ten on that ches'nut o' Brown's —
  He thinks mighty well o' his colt, I know,
An' I'd wager more only Fortune's frowns
  Have made my pile most mightily low.

I'm sorry, sir, that you're backin the mare;
  You should have seen *me* when you first came out.
I'll tell you the truth, an' you know I'm square:
  She isn't quite up to so long a route.
In a couple o' weeks or so, I think,
  Perhaps she'll be fit fer a bruisin' race.
Now, sir, after the chestnut wins, we'll drink,
  Fer ye know I'm backin' him straight an' place.

        .   .   .   .

Thar, darn it, they're off, an' my crimson sash
  Is away in the lead as sure as fate;
Looks like she'd gallop away wi' the cash.
  Come on thar, my honey! Come on, my Kate!
She wins in a gallop as sure's you're born !
  I hadn't a cent on her, as you see.
Why, she couldn't gallop a bit this morn,
  An' now she's won it, an' done fooled me.

BETTIE SIMPKINS' MARE.

Hidden deep in the Sierras, far below the peaks of snow,
Lay the little camp of Haley's in the summers long ago,
And the river that ran singing like a siren through the lands
Held a wealth of golden treasures deeply hidden in its sands.

Gold was god of all the miners, but their goddess was a girl,
Golden-haired and fair of feature, whom they'd christened
    " Little Pearl"—
Daughter she of Farmer Simpkins, owner of a plot of ground
Lower down within the valley, which he tilled the year around.

Suitors Bettie had a plenty, for the girl was wondrous fair,
But the only thing that won her was a little chestnut mare.
And all day among the mountains she was riding to and fro
'Mongst the pines that stood and whispered there below the peaks
    of snow.

Summers came and summers vanished, and the village grew
    apace,
And as older grew the village grew the girl in woman's grace.
Older, too, in strength and beauty grew the little chestnut mare
That was given o'er to Bettie and became the maiden's care.

Year by year the crops grew shorter; but the old man heeded not,
Till Necessity's stern mandate put a mortgage on the lot.
Then there entered Care and Trouble at the little cottage door —
Entered, too, the ghost of Famine — took its place upon the floor.

Naught knew Bettie of the trouble, until months had rolled away,
When the farmer, worn and weary, told her of their shortened
    stay
In the cottage; for the int'rest on the mortgage was unpaid,
And the sheriff only waited for the word to make his raid.

Bettie only smiled in answer, while the tears bedimmed her eyes,
Bent and kissed the old man lightly, like a woman worldly wise.

"God will help," she softly whispered; "He will heed a daughter's
    prayer."
Then went out and told her trouble to the little chestnut mare.

     .   .

Far away in quaint Sonora there was held a county fair,
And, to wager on the racing, gathered all the miners there;
But the great and chief attraction was a thousand-dollar race,
Free for all, to rule and harness, and 'twas this that filled the
    place.

These the entries that were given out in town the night before:
First the stallion Knight of Costa; then a gelding called The Moor;
Then the mare Queen of Sonora, and a gelding called Take Care:
Then a horse no one had heard of, entered Bettie Simpkins' mare.

When the race was called next morning and there rang the
    judges' bell,
Came there out four grizzled drivers, bowing to the miners' yell;
Then a boyish fellow followed with a jockey cap drawn down
O'er a fair and girlish forehead—he a stranger in the town.

Little time was lost in scoring, and the judges gave the word,
With the Knight of Costa leading and a-trotting like a bird.
Quickly sped he down the backstretch, followed closely by Take
    Care,
While, like death, upon his quarter hung the little chestnut mare.

In the stretch they swung together.   Knight of Costa soon was
    beat;
Then the mare made play for Take Care, and the gelding left his
    feet,
While she, coming strong and steady, passed beneath the judges'
    stand,
Winner of the heat in thirty, and still trotting well in hand.

The next heat the mare won easy, jogging in almost alone,
With the Knight of Costa distanced and his backers' money flown,
While the miners cursed and shouted, some in sorrow, some in joy,
And the baffled gray-haired drivers swore at fortune and the boy.

" *And she said, ' I'm Bettie Simpkins.'* "

When they went away the third time 'twas the Queen that showed
    the way,
With the Moor right at her throat-latch and the mare a length away;
And the watchers marked no changes till they squared away for
    home.
Then a shout came from the miners: " See the little chestnut
    come ! "

Trotting like a locomotive, soon she left behind the Moor,
And drew level at the distance with the Queen. " She'll win it,
 sure ! "
Yelled the miners; then they shouted, for the Queen had left her
 feet,
And the handsome little chestnut jogged in winner of the heat.

But the cheers gave place to silence, for about the judges' stand
Soon there gathered all the drivers, each a whip held in his hand,
And the spokesman of the party, he the driver of the Queen,
Claimed the chestnut mare had fouled him, as his partners all had
 seen.

First the judges heard in silence what the veterans had to say;
Then they asked the boyish driver to explain the tale away.
As he raised his cap to answer, down there fell a woman's hair,
And she said, "I'm Bettie Simpkins, and this Bettie Simpkins'
 mare."
Gazed the judges down in wonder at the maiden's flashing eyes,
While the other drivers, shamefaced, turned away in their
 surprise.
Then there came the quick announcement from the judges'
 watching-place:
" We give to Bettie Simpkins' mare the third heat and the race."
    .   .   .   .   .   .

There arrived a few days afterward at Farmer Simpkins' place
 The sheriff and his posse, and they found Miss Bettie there.
" Here's the money for your mortgage, sir; I won it on a race,"
 She said, "down at Sonora, where I drove my chestnut mare."

The old man looked down in wonder, and then, kneeling on the
 floor,
 He cried, "O God, I thank thee, and if racing be a sin,
I will promise thee my Bettie, Lord, shall never do it more.
 Thou knowest she was honest, and she drove the mare to
 win."

Soon a stranger came from 'Frisco who had heard about the
　　race,
Was introduced to Bettie, and he tried to buy the mare —
He offered a cool ten thousand; she declined the same with grace,
　　But still he kind of lingered, with his heart caught in her hair.
On sped the weeks with flying feet and found him lingering
　　there;
　　And then there came a wedding up at Farmer Simpkins' place.
The groom? That chap from 'Frisco. So I got the chestnut
　　mare,
　　But, better yet, the maiden that had driven her the race.

SHOWING THE THOROUGHBREDS.

(BELLE MEADE, OCTOBER, 1887.)

Belle Meade lay sleeping in the sun
　　That golden autumn day.
The live oaks wore their scarlet coats
　　And breeches lichen-gray.
The beech had changed its green attire
　　For dress of brown and gold,
And blue-grass pastures far away
　　In emerald billows rolled.

Beside the stables snowy white
　　The Nation's chieftain stood;
A woman, with her eyes alight,
　　Looked on in happy mood;
While Uncle Bob, a colored man,
　　With hair of silver gray,
Led out the gallant thoroughbreds
　　That make Belle Meade to-day.

" Dis yar hoss, Mistah President,
　　Am Bonnie Scotlan's son,
Ole Bramble. 'Spec's youh lady, sah,
　　Hab heerd how he could run.
He carried Dwyah's red and blue,
　　An', wid McLaughlin up,
He beat de bes' ones ob his day,
　　When racin fo' de Cup.

" This yar hoss, Mistah Presiden',
Am Bonnie Scotlan's son."

" Tak' kyeer dar, Mister President,
　　Don' get too clus his heels;
He don' mean nuffin' when he kicks,
　　Jes' shows how good he feels.
Dat leetle brown colt ober dar
　　Am one of Bramble's git;
'Specs, if dey gibs him half de chance,
　　He'll siah some racers yit.

" Dis chestnut heah am Enquiah;
    He's gettin' mighty old.
I reckon dat his get hab brought
    Dis fa'm his weight in gold.
From Californy to de Eas'.
    Whereber dey may be,
De boys all know ole Enquiah.
    De pride ob Tennessee.

" He 's daddy to de great Miss Foad,
    Dat carried Bal'win's cross
Up in Chicago, Derby Day,
    An' sulk, or couldn't los'
Dat great stake carried off by Todd.
    The mighty Egmon', too,
Am one of dis ole fellah's sons.—
    Heah! Stop, sah! Dat'll do.

" You needn't go to tear my clo'es,
    'Cause you's so mighty proud
Ob standin' foah de President
    An' dis uncommon crowd.
De lady wants to pat youh nose;
    Dat's right; stoop down your head.
Whoa, dar! Stan' mighty quiet now,
    An' show that you's well bred.

" Heah, sah, 's de king ob de whole lot,—
    Tak' ole Bob's word fo' dat,—
Luke Blackburn, jes' de gran'est hoss
    Dat eber trod de flat.
Jes' look, sah, at dat satin coat
    A-shinin' in the sun;
Look at dem powahful quahtahs, sah,
    An' say he couldn't run.

"Jes' let youh missus step dis way
    An' pat dis beauty's nose.
She likes a fin' hoss mos' as well
    As my gal do fine clo'es.
Dis hoss am mighty young as yit,
    But when he's had de chance
He'll hab some sons and daughtahs, sah,
    Dat's boun' to lead de dance.

"Dis brown one berry famous, sah—
    De mighty Iroquois;
He won de English Derby, sah,
    Much to de people's joy.
I t'ink sometime he toss his head
    About as if he knew
He mak' ole Englan' mighty sick
    Ob our red, white an' blue.

"He looks aroun' him mighty peert
    An sassy all de while;
He's t'inkin' 'bout de Prince of Wales—
    Dat mak's you'h lady smile.
He don' know you's de President,
    I specs he doesn't car';
He's berry English in his ways—
    Mus' larned em ober dar.

"Dis am, de las' one ob de lot,
    Great Tom, de English hoss,
Impoahted by de Gin'ral, sah,
    Who t'ought him jes' de hoss.
He ain't no berry great shakes, sah,
    Leas'wise dat I can fin'—
His sons and daughtahs, mos' ob dem,
    Hab allus run behin'.

" Dar, sah, you seen de mighty steeds
    Dat mak' Belle Meade to-day,
An' when you reads ob racin' deeds,
    Ef mem'ry turns dis way,
Jes' kin'ly t'ink ob Uncle Bob,
    De po' ole colored man
Youh visit to dis fa'm hab made
    De proudes' in de lan'."

THE PADDOCK GATE, AND HOW IT WAS OPENED.

Bring out my racing-jacket, Bob, and lay it on the bed;
    I'd like to put it on again, just once before I die.
Ah, many, many times, my lad, I've worn that blue and red;
    First past the post on Southern tracks, and 'neath a Northern
        sky.

You heard, lad, what the doctor said ? Nay, there's no need o'
    tears —
    I'll weigh out at the judges' stand, I reckon, Bob, all right.
I've never done a crooked act in all my forty years,
    And dying only means to sleep, to bid the world good-night.

I don't see how I fell to-day — I seemed to have it won.
    I never knew the big black colt to stumble, lad, before;
The favorite that Martin rode I had already done,
    And I saw the chestnut falter when we passed the stable door.

The gray was at my saddle-girths — I knew I had him beat,
    For Cunningham was urging him e'en then with whip and
        steel,
While I was sitting easy-like and quiet in my seat
    And humming o'er the music o' the old Virginny Reel.

"There's Saunderson! I thought him dead. By Jove! he's on The Lark!"

The track flew out behind me like a ribbon all unrolled;
  The hoofs made merry music as they echoed from the track;
The grand stand in the sunlight seemed a gleaming mass o'
      gold ;
  Then came a sense o' falling, and before me all grew black.

What happened then, I cannot tell!   It didn't hurt the black,
  The boys all say — and, lad, you know I'm mighty glad o' that.
That colt is bound to make his mark some day upon the track.
  The boys will find him bad to beat when racing on the flat.

Now move your chair up closer, lad.   You know my little Kate ?
  Her mother died ten years ago, ten years this very day.
Ah, me ! no man had ever yet a better running mate
  Than I until the angels came and carried her away.

The girl is like her mother, lad: the same brown hair and eyes;
  The self-same dimples in her cheeks; a laugh like silver
      chimes;
A heart as light as thistle-down that floats 'neath summer skies,
  Yet pure as is the virgin gold that comes from mountain mines.

Take her the papers in my chest — I've left to her the farm;
  This ring upon my finger here her mother used to wear —
And promise me that, while you can, you'll shield her safe from
      harm.
  I trust you as no other, lad; so make the lass your care.

Tell her, for she is rich, my lad, to use her riches well,
  For money makes not happiness, and riches oft take wings.
'Tis better in a cottage where Love sits enthroned to dwell
  Than to sit down with Indifference in a palace made by kings.

Why, Bob! I'm growing strangely weak — nay, leave the colors
      there:
  I'm going to take a little nap; I'll waken by and by.
"If I should die before I wake" — why! that's an infant's prayer!
  Lift up the curtains, lad, a bit; I wish to see the sky.

Turn up the light a little, Bob; it's getting mighty dark.
   Was that the saddling-bell that rang ? Come, hurry ! I'll be
     late.
There's Saunderson ! I thought him dead. By Jove ! he's on The
     Lark !
   Give me a hand. All ready, sir ! Swing wide the paddock
     gate.

The gate that opened no man saw. The angel at the bars
   Stood sentry while a jockey rode out on the silent track
That leads, so books and preachers say, to lands beyond the stars;
   But none who've ridden through that gate have ever yet come
     back.

"SCOTTY."

(Montana, 1885.)

" Scotty? " Yes, stranger, that's my hoss.
   How's he bred? Well, he's kind o' a cross
   'Tween Morgan stud an' a mustang mare.
   Looks like a Morgan? Well, now, I swear,
   Sometimes I think so, and then ag'in
   I can't see whar the good blood comes in.
   I raised him up from a suckin' colt,
   An' buckin' is nigh on his best holt.

Will I sell him? No, sir, stranger, no;
   Thar ain't gold enough on earth below
   To buy that hoss. Ye may think it strange,
   But I fancy that, when I cross the range,
   The Master 'll say: " Jim, you did well
   To keep that hoss, an' never to sell."
   And keep him 's what I intends to do,
   Long as thar 's forage enough for two.

He ain't wuth much ?   Not to you, perhaps.
That same remark has been made by chaps
As don't know nothin' about that hoss.
But better set down.   Thar 's a story, boss,
'Bout Scotty, an' as thar's nobody by,
I'll tell it — thank'ee, a little rye.
I never takes no sugar in mine;
Spoilin' good liquor ain't in my line.

" I saddled Scotty, and just as day
Broke o'er the mountains, I rode away."

One winter, nigh on five years ago,
When the roads was blocked with driftin' snow,
An' a blizzard swept the canyon here,
Till the old oaks' branches shrieked wi' fear,
The wife that I wed eight years ago,
Wi' her bronze brown hair an' her neck o' snow,
Were taken sick in the dead o' night,
An' us alone — not a soul in sight.

5

She grew wuss fast. When the mornin' come
It looked like life's sands most had run.
She whispered faint, "For God's sake, Jim,
Get the doctor here from the town o' Lynn."
I saddled Scotty, an' just as day
Broke o'er the mountains, I rode away,
An' as I went on I seemed to see
Her small white hands as they reached for me.

In just three hours, or a trifle more,
Perhaps, I had reached the doctor's door
An' told my mission. He shook his head —
"By the time I get there she 'll be dead;
For that hoss of mine is old an' slow,
An' he'll lose his way in the driftin' snow."
"Take Scotty, doctor; give him his head,
An' save my lassie," were all I said.

I watched him ride through the drifts away,
An' somehow, stranger, my lips would pray
That God would give Scotty strength an' speed
To save my wife in the hour o' need.
Then goin' out in the howlin' storm,
I foun' my way to the doctor's barn,
An' takin' his hoss, a spavined bay,
I saddled him up and rode away.

The night had covered the mountains o'er
Wi' sable cloaks when I reached the door
O' my cabin home, an' I could see
In fancy my wife's hands reached to me;
An' my heart stood still, all froze wi' dread,
As I thought perhaps she mought be dead.
I opened the door to find my wife —
An' a baby gal had crept to life.

The Doc had gotten thar sharp at nine;
He said himself he were just in time.
It mought have been 't was my whispered pra'r;
I'll always think it were Scotty thar;
An' though I knows it ain't etiquette
For a man to make his hoss a pet,
You can't have Scotty; no, not for gold.
The reason why—he ain't to be sold.

IN LUCK BOTH WAYS.

I tell you a tale that was told to me
  In the early dawn by a stable door,
While the moon that sank in the far-off sea
  Seemed to lift the dark from the sandy shore.
      It was told by a trainer old and gray —
      A Texas man — in a Texan's way.

"I hed a hoss called Butterball
   Some thirty years ago,
Seemed rather undersized an' small;
   He were a whirlwind though.
I never seed a hoss like him
   Afore or since that day
He galloped home a winner in
   The Autumn Cup.   Then Clay

"Allowed he were the grandest hoss
   Thet ever he hed seen;
An' offered me ten thousan' cash
   An' his mare, Betsy Green,
Ef I would sell him; but, you see,
   I wasn't sich a fool.
What does fer others does fer me,
   Has allers bin my rule.

"'T were way down South in New Orleans;
   Me an' my hoss waz thar,
A kind o' lookin' 'round fer greens,
   But runnin' on the squar'.
I 'd won a pesky purse er two,
   Enough to buy him oats,
But I 'd some bills a-comin' due,
   An' wasn't flush wi' notes.

"I 'd heerd about the Autumn Cup,
   An' entered Butterball.
I meant ef a good hoss kim up
   Ter never start et all.
I 'lowed ther forfeit I could pay
   Ef cracker-jacks kim in,
Then start ag'in some other day
   When sure that I could win.

"Two days afore the Cup waz run
   I giv my hoss a tri'l.
He fairly made the watches hum
   A-workin' thet three mile.
I sez, ' Jerusha,'—she's my wife—
   Er waz in them old days,
'Fore a divorce court crossed my life
   An' took her from my gaze,—

"I sez, ' Jerusha, sure ez sin,
   I'll win wi' Butterball.'
'Now, Tom,' sez she, 'ef you does win,
   I wants a hat this fall.'
Them waz her very only words,
   'Cept thet she added on
Bout wantin' et all trimmed wi' birds
   Ez had their feathers on.

" Et last ther Cup day kim along.
    Oh, Lord ! but I were blue,
Fer there were Sweetheart, owned by Strong,
    An' Makin's hoss, Ther Jew;
But, wuss than all, that feller Clay
    Hed entered Betsy Green,
An' somewhar from ther Texas way
    They'd brought down Prairie Queen.

" I 'lowed right off thet I were done,
    An' tried to draw ther hoss.
Ther judges wanted all ther fun,
    An' stated, mighty cross,
Thet I hed come along too late
    Ter draw my hoss et all;
They 'lowed I'd start ez sure ez fate
    Thet brown hoss, Butterball.

" Sez I, 'All right,' an' saddlin' up
    I sent him ter ther post.
'Now ef you wins ther Autumn Cup,'
    Sez I, 'yer jist a ghost;
But then I'll buy a pool, because
    Yer might win arter all.'
Three thousan' ter a hundred waz
    Ther odds gin Butterball.

" Now, right hyar's whar ther fun kim in.
    Them judges waz so smart;
My hoss went right along an' win —
    Upset their apple-cart.
He jumped out at ther fall o' flag,
    An' never stopped at all;
Thar wasn't nary single nag
    Ez got near Butterball.

"Thet night Jerusha — wife as waz —
    She kim an' said ter me,
'I wants thet new hat now, because
    Yer won the Cup, I see.'
'Hyar's jest a thousan' in cold cash,'
    I sez; 'don't spar' expense.'
She got ther hat, an' made er mash —
    I've never seen her sence.

"Et fust I felt most mighty bad
    Ter find out she hed gone;
The darkest hour, you know, 't is said,
    Is just afore ther dawn.
Since then I 'm happier in my mind;
    More peaceful are my days;
Ther Lord I think uncommon kind
    Ter send sich luck both ways."

OLD FREELAND.

They are schooling Freeland over the timber,
    Over the fences and walls of stone.
My heart flames up like a dying ember
    That burns in the darkness all alone;
And I fancy again, as I sit here dreaming,
    I hear the cheers from the crowded stand,
As they hailed him there in the sunlight gleaming,
    The grandest race-horse in all the land.

    Oh, turn him out in a field of clover —
        Out in the clover up to his knees;
    Now that his racing-days are over,
        Give him a life of lordly ease.

You have not forgotten that August weather —
Swiftly the picture comes back to me —
When he and Miss Woodford raced together
Down at the Branch by the sounding sea.
Oh, look at them now as the finish they're nearing,
Measuring swiftly each stride for stride.
Hark! don't you hear the wild Westerners cheering?
Freeland has won, by a queen defied.

" The grandest race-horse in all the land."

Oh, turn him out in a field of clover —
Out in the clover up to his knees;
Now that his racing-days are over,
Give him a life of lordly ease.

The great races he won will live in story
When you and I have been laid to sleep;
Others will tell of his vanished glory
When over our graves the grasses creep —

Tell how the bright red with blue sash of the Dwyers
　　Was trailed by him in the dust and clay;
How the green and white on the king of flyers
　　Led the great queen past the post that day.

　　Oh, turn him out in a field of clover —
　　　　Out in the clover up to his knees;
　　Now that his racing-days are over,
　　　　Give him a life of lordly ease.

He is crippled now and can race no longer;
　　His work is over, his mission done.
Then trouble him not on the race-track longer;
　　Let him gambol and dream in the sun.
Turn him loose in a field where the sunbeams quiver
　　In broken lances among the leaves;
Where the grass creeps down to the rushing river,
　　And reapers sing as they bind their sheaves.

　　Oh, turn him out in a field of clover —
　　　　Out in the clover up to his knees;
　　Now that his racing-days are over,
　　　　Give him a life of lordly ease.

THAT THOROUGHBRED NELL.

A TALE OF KENTUCKY IN 1863.

Did you ever hear tell of a brown mare called Nell,
　　That was bred in Kaintuck, on the old Ashland farm?
Of the race that she run and the stake that she won?
　　What! You haven't? Sit down, then; I'll spin you the yarn:

'Twas in June, sixty-three, and the hum o' the bee
　　Was a sound rarely heard about Lexington way,
For the rattling o' guns and the snarling o' drums
　　Made the most o' the music we heard ev'ry day.

In a little brown cot at the edge of a lot,
   On the old turnpike road that led down to the fort,
Where the shadows at dusk met to dance " Money Musk '
   To the whippoorwill's chorus, dwelt Jennie McCourt.

All 'round it the corn raised its spears to the morn,
   In spite o' the vandals in gray and in blue;
For the hollyhocks tall by the low garden wall
   Had witnessed two armies pass by in review.

Through that long summer day she could hear far away
   The low, thunderous growl of the big Parrott guns,
Till the echoes they woke rolled away in the smoke
   And came brokenly back in the snarl o' the drums.

In the fast-waning light, when 't was nearing the night,
   Blue-eyed Jennie crept out to the low cottage gate,
When a squadron in gray came swift riding that way,
   And then halted to camp there because it was late.

Now, among them rode one that was dear as the sun
   To the heart o' Miss Jennie — a prisoner, too.
He 'd one arm in a sling, like a bird's broken wing,
   An' a gilt eagle gleamed on his shoulder o' blue.

Then the girl she turned white as a ghost in the light,
   Though she spoke not a word to the prisoner there;
But the Lord, who heeds all to the sparrows that fall,
   Must have sent down an angel and answered her prayer.

When the camp-fire's red light burned a hole in the night,
   She crept out to the place where the wounded man lay,
'Neath a huge spreading oak, half concealed by a cloak,
   And she bound up his wounds in a woman's deft way.

" Mighty fond o' the Yanks," said the Johnnies. " What thanks
   Does yer ever expect that you'll get from them spies ? "

" Oh, I thought you were men," proudly answered she them,
  And I noticed a dangerous gleam in her eyes.

Then she whispered a word that the prisoner heard,
  And she threw him a kiss as she vanished away.
Not a Johnnie could see, though it looked plain to me
  There 'd be fun in that camp 'fore the dawn o' the day.

Then the moon came and went like a crescent that 's bent
  By some venturesome angel to sail through the skies,
While the stars, one by one, half in fear, half in fun,
  Peeped at earth through the smoke with their millions of eyes.

The lone guard at his post, to and fro, like a ghost,
  Paced out to the roadway, then back to the lane,
Where he paused to look down on the lights o' the town,
  Gave a shift to his carbine, and paced back again.

With a shadowy glide to the prisoner's side,
  All unseen by the sentry, crept Jennie McCourt.
" I 've a horse for you, dear, in the thicket quite near,"
  She low whispered.   " Come, mount her, and ride for the fort.'

Not a twig did they break, not a bird did they wake,
  As together they crept to the place where it stood;
Then she kissed him good-night, and with eyes all alight
  Watched him ride out alone to the edge o' the wood.

'T was that thoroughbred Nell that he mounted, and — well,
  'T was the flash of a carbine, an answering cheer,
Told the Johnnies that night o' their prisoner's flight,
  While a woman prayed God for his safety in fear.

Down the old turnpike road, with her crippled blue load,
  The wild thoroughbred dashed with the speed o' the wind —
Never stopping for breath, for the shadow o' death
  Followed swiftly on cavalry chargers behind.

" Down the old turnpike road, with her crippled blue load,
The wild thoroughbred dashed with the speed of the wind."

The gray dust, like a veil, from her mane to her tail
   Wrapped her close in its folds, and half hid her from sight,
While the white flecks o' foam ever backwards were blown
   As she sped, like a phantom, straight on through the night.

The farm watch-dogs would bark as we passed in the dark,
   While the farmer's wife muttered, "There 's foxes about,"
For how little she knew that a soldier in blue
   Was then riding a race for his life on that route.

Once a sentry in gray heard us coming his way.
   "Halt! Who goes there?" he shouted.   We dashed o'er the
      bridge;
Ere a musket could flash, with another wild dash
   We had vanished from sight o'er the top o' the ridge.

So all through the long night we kept up our wild flight,
   And the dawn o' the day found us safe at the fort.
I could never half tell all my thanks to Brown Nell;
   And I 've never ceased thanking sweet Jennie McCourt.

What 's become o' the mare? Well, she 's dead, I declare,
   But that brown colt down yonder is one of her sons.
Any good?   Why, great Scott! Not a horse in the lot
   Can beat him a-running.   He goes like great guns.

Oh, the girl?   On my life, I forgot.   She 's my wife,
   Though I never knew just why she cottoned to me.
We 've a family — four growing up 'round the door;
   That 's Miss Jennie, the second, you 've now on your knee.

THE HERO OF THE STABLES.

He was only a stable lad, was Jim, yet in his rugged breast
There beat a heart as tender and true as beats 'neath a velvet
vest.
He couldn't repeat, I'll stake my life, one o' the commandments
ten,
But he'd more religion 'neath his coat than you'll find in the most
o' men.

Born with a knowledge o' right and wrong that most o' men
acquire
For the simple reason they're afraid o' a brimstone lake o' fire,
He loved the children that played about as well as a miser gold,
Watched them as a shepherd does his sheep when the darkness
veils the fold.

Among the horses Jim had in charge was a stallion, big and
black,
As vicious a brute as ever set hoof, iron-shod, on a trotting-
track.
He had killed three men already there, an' nobody now but Jim
Dared enter the stall where he stood alone—the hoss seemed
fond o' him.

He rushed at strangers, open-mouthed, when they ventured to
near his stall;
The signs o' his temper showed in dents kicked deep in the hard
wood wall.
They'd christened him Satan. Well, indeed, he fitted that
dev'lish name,
Though in looks he were a beauty from his heels to his ebon
mane.

In the spring a little gal come out along wi' a chap from town
To see the horses. She'd eyes of blue an' hair of a golden
brown;

Though but six years old, she loved a horse as well as a woman
    can,
An' a woman loves a hoss, sometimes, far more than she does a
    man.

She'd pet them all with her dainty hands an' prattle in childish
    glee,
Till I seemed to hear the songs o' the birds an' streamlets laughin'
    free.

" In the dark o' Satan's stall."

Then I got to talkin' along wi' the chap o' old-time racin' ways,
O' politics an' a lot o' things as a feller will nowadays.

'T was all of a sudden we missed the gal, an', glancin' down the
    wall,
I caught the sheen o' her gold-brown hair in the dark o' Satan's
    stall.
My feet seemed glued to the old barn floor, an' my heart stood
    still in fright,
As I caught the flash o' that demon's eyes, like torches burnin'
    bright.

I thought o' the baby I had left in my far-off mountain home,
And tried to pray for the dainty gal that stood in that stall alone.
Then I saw that stable boy, that Jim, dash in through the open
    door
O' Satan's stall, an' the baby lay unharmed on the old barn floor.

Strong man as I am, I fainted then.   When back into life I came
Poor Jim lay there on the hay, a corpse, by that big black devil
    slain !
He 'd given his life for that little gal's.   A hero's act, you say ?
Aye, one that 'll give him a crown, I guess, when it comes to
    judgment day.

How did it happen ? God only knows.   It was only Him could see;
But I hope that never again on earth will terror come to me
Such as I felt when I saw that gal alone in that darkened stall
With the big black hoss, while Death's dark wings cast shadows
    over all.

He was only a stable boy, was Jim, yet in his rugged breast
There beat a heart as tender an' true as beats 'neath a velvet vest.
He couldn't repeat, I 'll stake my life, one o' the commandments
    ten,
Yet I reckon he 'll fare on judgment day better than most o' men.

HOW ROY WILKES DOWNED THE GANG.

I say, have you forgotten, lads, the race at Fleetwood Park,
When Davies captured all the cash between daylight an' dark,
While apples, Chinese-lantern-like, hung shining 'mongst the
    leaves,
An' shocks o' corn like pickets stood among the fallen sheaves ?
The day that Roy Wilkes downed the gang ?   Aye, that 's the day
    I mean.
Its memory still pursues me like the shadow of a dream.

Budd Doble had Ed Annan there, an' I remember well
That Herrington was pilotin' the roan mare Ulster Belle.
The little black mare Allen Maid was driven then by Trout,
While Turner, with Balsora Wilkes, thought he could beat Roy out.
Feeks o'er El Monarch held the reins.   I thought that he 'd gone
      daft,
When I saw Davies driving Roy, an' jest sat down an' laughed.

He surely had more cheek that day than any man I 'd seen,
To get out with a gang like that, an' him so pumpkin green;
For there 's a heap in driving, lads, as most o' folks allow;
There 's lots o' drivers all the time, an' but one Doble now.
I changed my mind some afterwards when loud the cheering rang
That greeted Roy, the stallion king, that day he downed the gang.

When warming up before the race, they made a pretty sight.
The tiny Allen Maid went by, a shadow o' the night;
The red roan coat o' Ulster Belle like burnished copper shone;
El Monarch seemed o' silver steel when he shot by alone;
Balsora Wilkes ungainly looked, but when Roy Wilkes came down
The track, a perfect storm o' cheers went up to greet the brown,

Who seemed a picture taken out from some old master's frame.
Folks thought Pegasus had come back to visit earth again.
His eyes flashed fire; he held his head aloft in kingly pride;
He seemed to spurn the very earth nor touch it in his stride.
He glanced about him right an' left, an' somehow seemed to say,
" I 'll prove that I am king, indeed, upon this track to-day."

The betting men were out in force that day at Fleetwood Park;
'T was fifty Roy an' fifty field.   I backed him for a lark.
I knew the horse was mighty fast — how fast I didn't know,
But thought when Davies held the reins he had but little show.
The gang would down him if they could, I knew as sure as fate,
An' so before I wagered much I thought it best to wait.

6

For Fortune, fickle jade at best, is full o' smiles and tears;
That plungers always come to grief 's the history o' the years.
The grandest-looking horse of all, that 's certain sure to win,
May break down when he 's way ahead an' be the last horse in.
Such thoughts as these passed through my mind; I said I 'd wait
        awhile,
Then wager more if Fortune seemed inclined that day to smile.

The first heat was an easy thing for Roy, it seemed to me.
He 'd Allen Maid an' Ulster Belle to keep him company.
He bade them good-by at the half, where watches marked "one
        four,"
Reluctant-like, as lovers leave their lassies at the door
When clocks chime out the wee sma' hours, an' stars begin to
        wane,
As though, to use an old song's words, the parting gave him pain.

Roy Wilkes now sold for fifty, while the field brought twenty-
        nine,
But Fortune, who had smiled before, put on a frown this time;
For Allen Maid cut in an' took the pole right at the word
An' flitted round the lower turn as swiftly as a bird.
The stallion jumped into the air — he made a tangled break
That sent him ten lengths to the rear — my heart began to ache.
The little black mare, pacing fast, climbed swiftly up the hill.
She beat Ed Annan home a length.   The crowd was hushed an'
        still.

Don't ask me where Roy Wilkes came in.   I didn't care to know.
I thought it was a hopeless task for him to win, an' so
I went an' hedged my money out by betting on the field.
I didn't know the heart o' oak that seal-brown coat concealed;
So, while the field brought twenty-five 'gainst twenty-two for
        Roy,
I placed three hundred in the box an' hugged myself for joy.

Just 'fore they started for this heat I glanced up at the stand
An' saw a red bandana waved in some tall fellow's hand;
Then, turning quick, saw Davies nod his head, an' like a flash
The thought came to me: Roy will win; they've got on all their
  cash.
I tried to hedge my money out, but didn't have a chance,
For every time they came to score that stallion led the dance.

The Maid, the Belle an' Roy all swung round the first turn in
  line;
A blanket would have covered all the three at any time.
Then, as the stallion forged ahead, he once more left his feet,
An' Allen Maid shot to the front — I thought she 'd win the heat.
But no ! The horse soon caught again — he rallied with a will
An' set sail for the leaders who were climbing up the hill.

The sulky-wheels seemed flashing rims — the spokes were lost
  to sight;
He danced along as shadows dance across the face o' night.
He soon passed all but Allen Maid. Trout thought he had it
  won,
When suddenly a flying shape dashed by him in the sun
That gilded o'er the Point o' Rocks, an' quicker than a flash
Those drivers realized that Roy 'd a mortgage on the cash.

'T was all in vain. Balsora Wilkes was hurried through the
  straight
To catch that stallion from the West, who 'd struck at last his
  gait.
You 've seen an engine flash along the narrow rails o' steel,
While all the mile-posts, painted white, behind it dance a reel;
You 've seen a whirlwind sweep across a meadow, daisy-grown —
So swept Roy Wilkes along the track, an' finished all alone.

An' now the odds were three to one on Roy, the takers few.
Old General Turner an' the gang were feeling mighty blue:

They'd all their money in the box, and couldn't get it out;
They knew that Roy could beat them then the whole length o'
    the route.
When scoring up he seemed to say, as plain as plain could be,
"Although I know I'm handicapped to-day, you can't beat me."

The race was all but over then.   Roy went away so fast,
The instant they received the word, that, when the half was
    passed,
He led his field an open length, an' going up the hill
He seemed, with every single stride, to draw off further still.
He then jogged home just as he pleased, while loud the cheering
    rang,
For, single-handed and alone, Roy Wilkes had downed the gang.

How fast were those four heats ? you ask.   The fastest ever made
At Fleetwood by a pacing horse; an' yet he only played
With that whole field, an' beat the gang in such an easy way,
It seemed he might have distanced all who met him there that
    day.
I'll gamble now a horse that meets an' beats him anywhere
Can give Maud S. a rattling race—an' she's no common mare.

MISS WOODFORD.

QUEEN OF THE TURF.

Kentucky-born, Kentucky-bred,
A beauty from her heels to head,
I see her in my dreams again,
The daughter of old Fancy Jane
And Billet, as she stood that night,
A picture in the waning light,
Nor dreamed a queen she crowned should be,
With laurels, by the sounding sea.

I see her led into the ring,
Fit daughter of the harem's king.
With quiv'ring nerves and flashing eyes
She looks around in calm surprise.
I hear the auctioneer explain
Her breeding: "Billet—Fancy Jane."

" The daughter of old Fancy Jane and Billet."

The bidding lags—the filly's sold,
Bought by the Dwyers' yellow gold.

The years drift by, and once again,
With throbbing heart and reeling brain,
I see a great race run and won
At Monmouth 'neath a burning sun.
I see them gather at the post;
I see that filly or her ghost.

"They 're off," the caller loudly cries —
I follow them with straining eyes.

I hear the sound of rattling hoofs
Like rain-drops beating on the roofs,
And catch the flash of colors bright,
Like comets hurled across the night;
I hear again through all the years
The music of the deafening cheers
That rise and fall and die away
As does the tide on Fundy's Bay.

The hurrying hoofs draw nearer yet.
The jockeys' teeth are firmly set;
The racers, straining every nerve,
Like shadows sweep around the curve.
The colors, shifting as they run,
Look like a rainbow in the sun,
And cracking whips make music dear,
With jingling spurs, to turfman's ear.

The flying feet come nearer still;
'T is like the clatter of a mill,
That changes to a rolling drum,
As down the stretch the racers come.
I hear men shout above the din:
"Come on. the black!" "The gray will win!"
The dust is flying like a cloud —
The horses hidden in a shroud.

Look quick! the dust is backward blown;
They 're just a furlong now from home.
A brown mare leads the broken ranks;
A chestnut hangs upon her flanks.
The frenzied racers rush and reel
Beneath the sting of whips and steel.

Now ride, McLaughlin! ride for life —
So won young Lochinvar a wife.

The brown comes on with giant strides;
She feels the master hand that guides.
Though slender legs begin to tire,
She struggles on to reach the wire.
The chestnut falters and falls back;
The brown comes on and takes the track.
"Miss Woodford wins!" I hear the cheer,
And crown her queen of all the year.

Beyond the mountains, where unrolled
The wheat-fields lie in sheets of gold,
When ripened by the summer sun,
And silver streamlets laughing run,
Miss Woodford wanders. By her side
A filly plays — the Haggin pride —
To prove in after days, I ween,
The worthy daughter of a queen.

A COLORED TIP.

(DIXIANA, FEBRUARY, 1886.)

I 's an ole Kaintucky niggah, an' fo' nigh on fifty yeah
I 's been workin' fo' de Majah on de ole plantation heah,
An' I 's watched de colts an' fillies as dey 'd kick aroun' an' run,
When de blue grass hid deir fetlocks whar it rippled in de sun.

I kin 'member when de Majah was a younga' man dan now,
Foah dem debbles Care an' Trebble cut deir furrows in his brow;
When he put above de gate-way, in big lettahs dat war cl'ar:
"Dar's no peddlers an' no nuffin' but a race-hoss wanted hyar."

Da's been many a good race-hoss dat war raised upon dis farm.
Hyar dat streak ob lightnin', Punster, an' de great Ban Fox war
    born.
Hyar de King Bans lib in clober till we sen' dem off to sell,
An' dey dons de silks an' satins fo' to mak' de people yell.

Ober yondah stan's ole Himyah, an' I 'members well de day
Dat dat ole hoss win de Merchants', an' I's heerd ole Majah say
Dat afore he done went broke down he war jes' about de boss,
Like ole Freelan' am in dese days, an' no common kin' ob hoss.

See dat filly standing yondah an' a-nibblin' at her hay;
Bettah keep youh eye upon her if she starts on Derby Day.
Bettah watch Sis Himyah, massa, when she starts for any race;
Bettah play her sure an' sartin — play her straight and play her
    place.

Kin she beat Ban Fox? No, massa, not if dat King Ban am right.
He kin beat the whole caboodle in dat race cl'ar out ob sight.
Ole Jack Chinn, afore he sold him, tole me time an' time agin
Dat dat colt, ef rightly ridden, beat de debbil, suah as sin.

Dar, I's done bin gone an' done it. Majah says I talk too much.
Beats ole Nick my tongue gets runnin' when I talks ob colts an'
    such.
He gets mad an' scolds dis niggah when I hasn't done jes' right;
Den he han's me out a dollah, 'foah de sun 's done gone at night.

Freedom? What I want of freedom when I 's happy whar I am,
Libbin' like a bee in clober — workin', too, fo' such a man?
You kin tak' youh 'Mancipation Proclamation to de ryar —
" Dar's no peddlers an' no nuffin but a race-hoss wanted hyar. "

FORBIDDEN FRUIT;

OR, How Flying Cloud was Saved.

I.

Jimmy, Bill has passed his checks in, and has gone across the
    range
To a place thar ain't no hosses, to a country that is strange;
But he left good deeds behind him.   Could a poet these discern —
Put them down in homely phrases—then his fellow-men might
    learn
That there's men with hearts as honest in the shadow of a stall
As there is around the churches where the steeples' shadows fall.

II.

Bill was nothing but a rubber; bin with hosses all his life;
Liked the sense o' bein' lonely; hadn't either child or wife;
Used to whisper to the hosses like he thought they'd understand
Everything he tried to tell them, while with hard yet gentle
    hand
He would braid their manes with ribbons and would smooth their
    glossy coats;
See that each one had its water, see that each one had its oats.

III.

In the stable where Bill labored was the trotter Flying Cloud;
He'd a record in the twenties, though the most o' folks allowed
He could trot a good deal faster if he had to trot to win.
Some said he could beat the devil, though that saying were a sin.
He were Bill's partic'lar fancy, just the apple o' his eye,
An' he watched him mighty closely when he saw a stranger nigh.

IV.

'T was in eighty, down in Boston; Flying Cloud was entered there
In the free-for-all for stallions, an' I often heard Bill swear

There was nary hoss to beat him, not one as could make him trot.
Even though some mighty good ones had been entered in the
lot.
I had seen him up the country win in time I thought was slow,
But I never took his measure; didn't know how fast he'd go.

V.

'T was the night before the big race, when two strangers went to
Bill,
Offered him ten thousand dollars if he'd work the stallion ill —
Give him just a little somethin' that they'd furnish there an' then.
"No," said Bill, "I wouldn't do it if you'd make it ten times
ten."
An' that night he moved his blankets to the stallion's stable,
where
He could watch the hoss an' find out if they meant him mischief
there.

VI.

It was shortly after midnight. Bill was lost in other scenes.
Ghosts of trotters long departed chased each other through his
dreams,
Smashing records all to flinders; for it's strange the time they
keep
When they send along their horses in the magic land of sleep.
Bill was wakened by the creakin' of a window in the wall,
While a little streak o' moonlight darted crosswise o' the stall.

VII.

Then he lay and watched the window till he saw a face appear
At the opening, when his pistol rang out loud an' sharp an' clear;
An' he heard a curse low muttered an' the noise o' flyin' feet
That the echoes seemed to waken all along the moonlit street.
Blades o' grass beneath the window showed some splashes here
an' there
That were crimson in their color, but nobody seemed to care.

" Flying Cloud don't get no apple 'fore this race, you understand !"

VIII.

The next morning, some time after Bill had rubbed the stallion
  down,
There come looking through the stables quite a party from the
  town,
An' among them was a woman just as pretty as a peach
Such as school boys always long for when they 're hangin' out o'
  reach.
She just plied old Bill with questions, that he answered mighty
  cross;
From her pockets took an apple that she offered to the hoss.

IX.

But Bill quickly snatched the pippin from the dainty creature's
  hand —
" Flying Cloud don't get no apple 'fore this race, you under-
  stand!"
Was his muttered exclamation; an' he added, speaking low:
"Apples just raised hell with Adam once in Eden long ago."
Flushed the woman to her temples as she quickly turned away,
While beneath her jetty lashes lightning seemed to flash and
  play.

X.

Flying Cloud that day in Boston won a race you should have
  seen;
Beat Don Juan and fourteen others — trotted there in two-thirteen,
While his party made a killing. They had every ticket sold
On the stallion that Dame Rumor made the fastest ever foaled;
But the proudest man around there was old Bill, who led him
  back,
Crowned the king of trotting stallions from his triumph on the
  track.

XI.

That same night, as we sat smoking by the open stable door,
Telling tales of old-time races like we 'd often done before,
Bill remarked, "Guess I was foolish 'bout that apple, Tom, to-day.
Angels never pizen hosses, an' I reckon 't aint their way,
But you see, lad, I were narvous 'bout the hoss, an' anyhow,
Men can't be too mighty careful in this business, you 'll allow.

XII.

"I were mighty fond o' apples when a lad, I were myself,
An' that pippin looks so temptin', as it lays thar on the shelf,
That I reckon I shall eat it just afore I goes to bed.
Want a piece?"   I don't eat apples, so I only shook my head.
Then the moon rose o'er the hill-tops, while the shadows shorter
          grew,
An' I said "Good-night" an' left him, for I 'd still some work to do.

XIII.

Jimmy, Bill did eat that apple. When we called him at the dawn,
He were sleepin', but his spirit somehow 'd taken wings an' gone.
Heart disease, the doctors called it, for them doctors never knew
O' this tale about the pippin that I 'm spinning here to you.
But if Bill could only spoken; if those lips, so still an' mute,
Could have moved, he 'd made the verdict: "Cause o' death —
          forbidden fruit."

WHY THE CAPTAIN QUIT RACING.

AN OLD TURFMAN'S STORY.

Will I join you ?   What ?   In a glass o' wine ?
No, none o' your new fancy drinks in mine !
Rye whisky an' sugar 's the drink for me,
But wine an' my stomach never 'll agree,
An' I 'm gettin' too old to change now'days,
For old dogs, you know, hate to learn new ways.
Wine may do now for young men o' your wealth,
But I 'll stick to my whisky.   Here 's your health !

You were talkin' hoss when I wandered in —
About Proctor Knott an' the bay Galen —
An wonderin' which was the best to play,
The big chestnut colt or the gallant bay.
Well, you might stand right there an' argufy
As to which was best till the day you die,
An' the chances are you wouldn't agree
Any more than you does about wine with me.

For there 's nothin' sure in the racin' line,
An' racin' hosses is losin' good time
Unless you can race for the sport alone,
An' back only hosses you call your own.
Then you 're often wrong, as I ought to know.
What — tell you the story ? Oh, pshaw, boys, no !
Well, sit down with me by this blazin' fire,
And for once I 'll give you your hearts' desire :

It was down in old Kentucky, many, many years ago,
Where the sweet magnolias blossom in the spring-time white as
    snow;
Where the blue grass pastures stretch away beneath the old oak
    trees,
And roses, blushing, bend their heads beneath the amorous breeze.

I 'd sixteen hosses in my string; the likeliest one o' all,
A big bay mare by Boston, known as Nancy Afterall.
I 'd been winnin' lots o' races, an' was flyin' sort o' high
Owned the earth, an' was just tryin' for a mortgage on the sky.

Nancy Afterall was entered in an all-aged sweepstakes race,
An' I thought that she could win it, but was sure she 'd get the
    place:
So I put Dan Rogers on her with instructions: "Take the track
When the flag falls, an' just keep it, never turnin' to look back."

There were just eleven hosses that stood grouped about the post.
Rogers' face was white as ashes, an' he looked more like a ghost
Than a livin' human being. Suddenly the flag went down,
An' the race began in earnest; but the leader was Jack Brown.

'T was in vain I looked for Nancy an' my colors blue and white.
They had vanished as completely as a fallin' star at night,
An' I never knew what happened till the race was run and won.
Then I tumbled to the racket, an' I knew that I 'd been done.

I had backed the mare for thousands, both to win an' for a place,
An' had Rogers rode to orders I 'd have never lost the race.
But he never tried to win it, and the starter, Parson Bill,
Told me she was left a-standin' when the flag fell, standin' still.

I was mad, an' you can gamble that I ripped around and swore;
But that didn't save my money, an' I vowed I 'd race no more.
So I went an' sold my hosses — sacrificed 'em for a song.
Now I never back a race-hoss though I do not think it wrong.

Them that likes can bet on races; as for me, I 've jumped the game.
Rather buck against the tiger, though I say it to my shame.
If the jockeys all were honest, an' the racin' always square,
There 'd be more men ownin' hosses; there 'd be fewer men that
    swear.

BURTON'S
PRAIRIE BELLE;

Or, How the Cup was Run and Won.

Have you ever read the story,
    or heard anybody tell
Of how once the cup was run and won by Burton's Prairie Belle?
A little scrawny chestnut mare, with a golden tail and mane,
That, whene'er she cut the sunshine through, seemed bannerets
    o' flame.
Oh, a gamer race was never run — I 'm willing now to swear
That there never was so game a hoss nor half so game a mare.

It was on a Southern race-track an' nigh twenty years ago;
It was drawin' close on to winter, an' the air was full o' snow.
I had a hoss called Eagle, a big, powerful-looking gray,
That was raised in old Kaintucky, an' was bred to run an' stay;
It cost *me* a cool two thousand just to enter for the cup,
But I thought my hoss could win it, an' I put my money up.

There were six that faced the starter, an' the night a-comin' on;
They were at the post a moment — in another they were gone.
My gray hoss went out and took the track.　He set so fast a pace
He had that field o' six strung out in the first mile o' the race;

7

He led them by three open lengths when they galloped by the
　　stand,
An' next him came Burton's chestnut mare, both runnin' well in
　　hand.

The second time they passed the stand my gray was leadin' still.
It seemed like he ought to leave the mare just at his jockey's
　　will.
They had run two miles already then an' still had two to go.
I caught the flash o' my scarlet sash — a fire-fly's signal glow.
I felt the hush o' the multitude, then heard somebody yell:
"My God, the chestnut's collared the gray — see Burton's
　　Prairie Belle!"

The tale was true — a mile to go — they were racin' side by side,
To music made by whip an' spur, a-measurin' stride for stride.
They sped away 'round the lower turn an' down the backstretch
　　flew.
They looked from the stand a single hoss — you'd never dreamed
　　o' two.
I felt the cold sweat runnin' down my back like drops o' rain.
A sixteenth out she faltered a bit, then gamely came again.

The gray was straining every nerve, but Burton's mare was game.
Three times she seemed a-givin' it up, then came with a rush again.
The air was full o' men's flyin' hats; cheers flew about like hail;
The mare was comin' along outside, my gray hoss next the rail.
In the last few strides she forged ahead; then, staggering, lurched
　　and fell.
Dead under the wire — a winner, too — lay Burton's Prairie Belle!

THE DRIVER'S STORY.

(TEXAS, 1880.)

Yes, sir; I 've been drivin' hosses now for nigh on twenty year,
An' I 've seen some funny races, that the crowd thought mighty
queer;
An' jest once I handled ribbons when I really felt afraid —
I were drivin' old Snap Dragon in a race 'gin Limpin' Maid.

It were 'way down south, in Texas, whar the boys air on the shoot,
Carry pistols in their pockets, an' a bowie in their boot,
An' they had a heap o' money on the mare an 'gin the hoss,
'Cause, I guess, they sort o' reckoned that the Limpin' Maid were
boss.

'T were a match, an' the conditions were the best two out o' three,
An' the stakes they were five thousand — pretty big they looked
to me.
Well, I won the first heat easy, sort o' come home in a jog;
Looked to me I 'd take the money, just like rollin' off a log.

Out thar stepped a long lank cowboy, just as I were coolin' out,
An' says he to me, " Say, stranger, what in thunder you about?
Me an' my pards has our money in the pool-box on the mare.
If she loses you 're a-goner, for we 're bound to raise your hair. "

" Well," says I, my dander risin' as I kind o' sized the game,
" You can bluff me, but I 'm winnin' wi' Snap Dragon all the same. "
When he left me he were ugly, but I didn't budge an inch,
Though I saw he thought I 'd weaken when it came down to the
pinch.

Both of us were goin' level when the starter giv' the word,
But I beat her goin' easy 'round the first turn like a bird,
Drew away along the backstretch farther still, an' squared for
home,
When I heard the crowd a-yellin', an' I kinder heaved a groan.

"For," says I, "I'll be a dead man when I reach the judges' stand,
An' I haven't got no mortgage on the parson's promised land."
But I kept the hoss a-goin'— I were twenty lengths or more
'Head o' Limpin' Maid, I reckon, when I went across the score.

When I passed the wire, such yellin' as thar was — 't would split
an ear.
Then thar come the sound o' pistols firin' rapid in my rear,
An', a-turnin' in my sulky, what I saw, on lookin' 'round,
Were the Limpin' Maid's tall driver lyin' dead upon the
ground.

What? The reason why it happened? Well, it's simple as can
be:
Them air fellows thought that driver had been sellin' out to me;
So they sorter had a reck'nin', an' 'fore he could use his lips,
They had dealt a brace game on him, an' had gathered in his
chips.

They were fools. Why, old Snap Dragon could have beat the
mare that day,
Hitched to sulky or to wagon, or in any kind o' way.
Oh, I had a great reception when I went their way again!
Though they thought I were dishonest, yet they 'lowed that I
were game.

BOB AIKEN'S RIDE TO DEATH.

AN OLD OWNER'S STORY.

Did I know little Aiken, the jockey? Why, you bet I did,
stranger, o' course.
No, he wasn't no rider like Murphy, but then there were many
lots worse —
He'd a rattlin' good seat an' was honest — that's somethin' ye
can't say o' all;
An' he wasn't afraid, sir, o' nothin', although he'd had many a fall.

I fust saw the lad down in Texas; he were ridin' a racer called
    Belle,
That was fast as a shot — for three-quarters her owners allowed
    she were hell.
An' I 'd made 'em a match for five hundred, for I had a hoss o' my
    own
That I knowed was as quick as chain-lightnin' — a geldin' I 'd
    christened Shoshone.

I 'm not goin' to tell ye the story about that are race, for it 's old,
An' ye know that such tales become chestnuts when they has
    been many times told;
But I lost both my hoss an' my money; my boy was outrode in
    the dash,
And that Belle, with that feller, young Aiken, just galloped
    plumb off with the cash.

Then we met — it was several years after — at Louisville, late in
    the fall;
He was ridin' my hoss in the Merchants', a long-stridin' bay they
    called Saul.
There was thirty to one up against him 'fore ever he went to the
    post;
An' Bob Aiken looked sick and discouraged; his face was as
    white as a ghost.

The race was the fourth on the programme, an' the day it was
    rainy and cold,
While the fog like a pile o' gray blankets across the green fields
    had been rolled.
But at last all the hosses were saddled, an' twelve o' them went
    to the post.
Gray Nance was the choice o' the talent, an' o' money she carried
    the most.

When I helped young Aiken to saddle he complained o' a pain in
  his side;
But he reckoned he knew his own business, and swore he were
  able to ride.
Yet my heart kind o' stood in my throat as I watched him slow
  gallop away.
His face looked as white as a gravestone loomin' up through the
  mist cold an' gray.

They stood grouped at the post but a moment. The fog hid the
  start from our view.
As they dashed by the stand we could see 'em, and leadin' the
  field was True Blue;
Gray Nance hangin' right on his quarter, while the very last hoss
  of 'em all
Was that long-stridin' bay o' Bob Aiken's, the pride o' my stable,
  that Saul.

They was gone from sight in a moment, an' we heard but the
  hurryin' hoofs
That kept on a-makin' sweet music, like the sound o' the rain on
  the roofs.
Down the backstretch, a ghostly procession, they sped through
  the mist an' the rain;
Then they circled the turn and were nearing the wire an' the
  grand stand again.

First I heard a faint cheer in the distance that came from the stables,
  I knew.
Then they cried out, " The favorite 's beaten ! " " Go on there,
  you coon, with True Blue ! "
Then out from the fog, like an arrow — by Jove, he was leadin'
  'em all —
Emerged the white face o' Bob Aiken, who was ridin' my long-
  stridin' Saul.

"Must I weigh in the corpse? For the jockey that rode Saul, the winner, is dead!"

Coming on steady as clock-work, he won by two lengths at the
    stand,
But the jockey made never a movement; he stirred not a foot or
    a hand.
When the hoss, stopping up on the turn, sir, came back to the
    weighing-out place,
Little Aiken sat lookin' afore him with a mark as o' death on his
    face.

I spoke, but he answered me not, sir; then I touched him an',
    "Judges," I said,
"Must I weigh in the corpse? For the jockey that rode Saul, the
    winner, is dead!"
"Aye, aye," come the sorrowful answer; so we weighed him an'
    found it all right.
There the game lad lay dead, an' me richer by ten thousand dol-
    lars that night.

THE DEACON'S PURCHASE.

The Deacon sat down in his easy-chair.
    "Good wife," said he, "I have been to town,
Where the people are holding the county fair,
    And I went to see it with Deacon Brown.
There were peaches there as big as your head,
And apples, rosy and round and red;
But the nicest thing of 'em all to me
Was a big bay mare that I chanced to see.

"But she were a beauty. and no mistake,
    And she stood, I reckon, full sixteen hands;
She trotted her heats with never a break,
    An' turned at a touch o' the driver's hands.
An' I say, good wife, you needn't be cross,
But I out with the dust, an' bought that hoss,

And now, going to church or coming home,
We 'll take no dust, for we 'll travel alone."

" Now, Lor' sakes !" said the good old wife; " but, my !
    The Deacon 's crazy, and no mistake."
And she uttered a long-drawn, heartfelt sigh,
    As she thought of Methodist rules he 'd break
By going to church at a break-neck speed,
And driving a trotter — awful deed.
She fancied herself on the anxious seat
Of his one-hoss shay in the crowded street.

When the Sunday came it was warm and bright,
    And the Deacon hitched up his big bay mare,
And lifted his wife to the seat as light
    As a cavalier — while she breathed a prayer.
Then hurried away down the village street,
While his wife held on to the anxious seat;
And the people stood on the walk to stare
As he hurried past with his big bay mare.

The parson attempted to drive 'longside
    With his sorrel mare and his one-hoss shay.
A touch of the whip, and the parson's pride
    Was left in the distance far away.
The livery man with his brand-new rig
Was left in the shade by the Deacon's gig,
And even the good wife smiled in church
As she thought how all were left in the lurch.

HOW WILD ROSE WON THE CUP.

A TRAINER'S STORY.

You have heard, I suppose, of a mare called Wild Rose,
    That was bred at Belle Meade, down in old Tennessee;
How she ruined young Brown once by beating The Clown
    And a host of good horses when ridden by me.

What! You ain't? On my word, now, that's really absurd,
    For that race made a wonderful stir in its day.
On an old Southern course it was run, and lots worse
    Have I seen since I flung my old jacket away.

'T was a long time ago, ere the frost and the snow
    Had both sifted and drifted deep into my hair.
I was riding for Gray, whom I 've often heard say:
    " He can ride like the devil when chased by a prayer."

'T was a race for the cup, and you bet up and up,
    With five hundred a corner to enter and run.
There was Giles' Mickey Free and Bill Bird's Busy Bee,
    Jimmy Adams' mare Nance and Tom Burton's Gray Nun.

There was Featherly's Kate, and a horse called the Mate,
    That was brought up from Texas on purpose to start;
Then that bay horse The Clown, that belonged to Jim Brown,
    And a gray from Kaintuck that was known as The Dart.

To these eight at the post add Wild Rose and The Ghost —
    The latter a slashing big black, owned by Marr,
With a mane and a tail like a lady's crepe veil,
    And a little white spot on his face like a star.

My instructions were few: " Just look out for those two,"
    Said old Gray, and he mentioned The Ghost and The Clown.
" If the pace ain't too strong let the mare rate along;
    Then come on at the finish, and cut them all down."

"That 's all right, sir," I said, as I nodded my head;
  Then I saw the flag fall, and the race had begun.
We were all well abreast —though just leading the rest
  By a scant head and shoulders was Burton's Gray Nun.

'T was an old-fashioned dash of four miles for the cash,
  And the pace was a burster —too fast from the start;
So I took the mare back as she strode o'er the track,
  Till I found myself eighth and alongside The Dart.

When the first mile was done we had settled Gray Nun,
  While Nance, too, was in trouble, and so was The Mate.
Busy Bee with Young France was now leading the dance,
  And right up to his throat-latch was Featherly's Kate.

When two miles had been passed the Gray Nun boys were last,
  And 't was Featherly's Kate showed the way by the post,
While next to her The Dart, running strong as at start,
  Showed just barely a throat-latch in front of The Ghost.

In the next half we ran racing really began,
  And back into the ruck there dropped Featherly's Kate,
While that gray horse, The Dart, showed a touch of faint heart,
  And old Wild Rose was gaining as steady as fate.

As we dashed by the stand the wild notes of a band
  Floated faint to my ears as The Ghost led the way,
While the patter of hoofs, like the rain on the roofs,
  Woke the echoes heard after for many a day.

As we raced 'round the turn I could scarcely discern
  The low stables that seemed to sail by on the wind,
But, half turning my head as still onward we sped,
  I saw The Clown coming up swift from behind.

We'd a quarter to go, and we rocked to and fro,
  With The Clown at my throat-latch and I at The Ghost's,

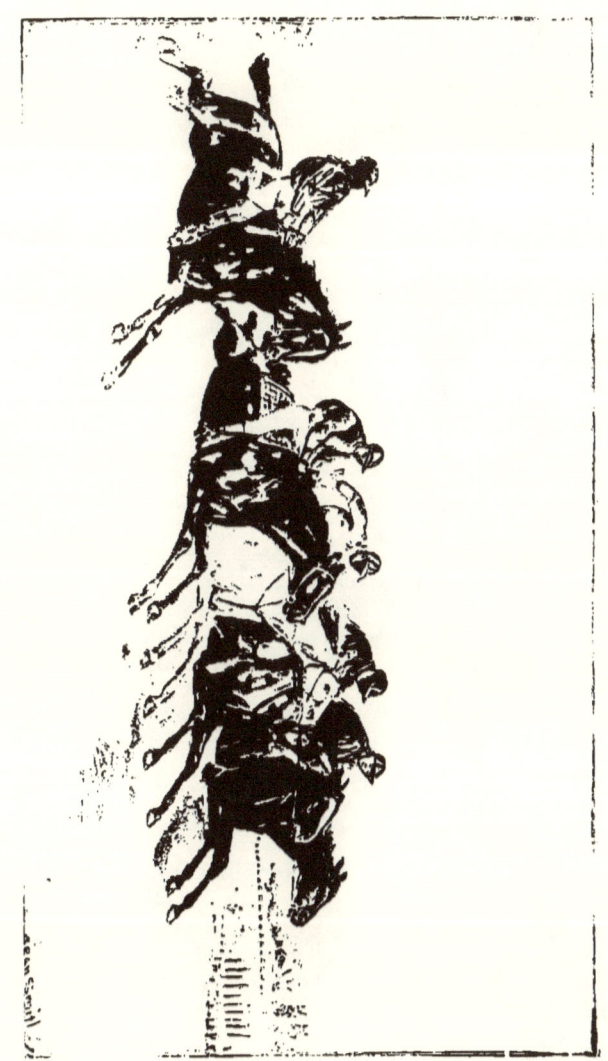

While the white flecks of foam that swift backwards were blown
  To my fancy seemed bubbles blown back at the posts.

The Ghost faltered a bit — he was too game to quit,
  And old Wild Rose was showing the way by a nose.
Then I brought my whip down, and she shook off The Clown
  As before me the stand and the judges arose.

Good God! How she'd reel as I gave her the steel!
  "The Ghost wins! The Ghost!" echoed over the track.
Two red nostrils flashed fire as I turned in my ire,
  And there coming again was that demon the black.

It was rock, it was reel, it was whip, it was steel,
  As first one, then the other, would show in advance.
Oh! my blood seemed on fire as we swept 'neath the wire —
  Had The Ghost or Wild Rose finished first in the dance?

When I rode back to weigh in the sunshine that day,
  I was greeted by deafening cheers from the stand,
For "Wild Rose by a nose!" was the verdict of those
  Who could see, and I felt like a king in the land.

THE BITERS BIT.

A BALLAD OF BRIGHTON BEACH.

At Brighton, by the ocean deep,
  Beside the sandy track,
At sunset on a summer's day,
Two trainers close together lay,
  The green grass at their back.

The sunbeams danced among the leaves
  Like fairies shod with light,
And over by the stable door
There stood a dozen steeds or more —
  It was a goodly sight.

" I say, John," quoth the younger man,
   With laughter in his eyes,
" I 'll have Jerusalem pull the mare,
  Then you can win with Captain Clare;
   The public we 'll surprise."

" All right, Bill," answered back his friend:
  " I think that scheme will go,
The mare 'll be favorite, of course,
And I 'll jump in and back the horse,
  While you can just lay low."

" *Two trainers close together lay.*"

They shook hands o'er the compact made,
  Then whistling walked away,
Nor dreamed that fate could have in store
A thing that should surprise them more
  Than any seen that day.

Next day, among the thoroughbreds
  That faced the starter's flag,
Conspicuous was a big bay mare,
And right beside her Captain Clare,
  And next a sorrel nag.

The flag went down. They jumped away,
    The Captain in the van.
The bay mare couldn't run a yard,
Jerusalem held her back so hard,
    But, Lord ! the sorrel ran.

They circle round the sandy track;
    They 've passed the half, and still
The sorrel 's at the Captain's girth !
John's eyes have lost their look of mirth,
    And William, too, is still.

Ho ! Clear the track ! They 're coming home;
    Great Scott ! is that a ghost ?
By heavens ! it 's the sorrel mare,
A neck ahead of Captain Clare;
    She 's nipped him on the post.

.   .   .   .

At Brighton, by the ocean deep,
    Beside a sandy track,
Two trainers cursed, as trainers will
Who 've lost their wealth; then all was still,
    The green grass at their back.

The moral of my tale is plain:
    Dishonesty don't pay;
One better have the best horse win
Than let a rank outsider in
    To steal the purse away.

IN MEMORIAM.

(Dan Mace, Died 1885.)

" I 'm trotting my last great race," he said,
    This wrinkled driver with locks of gray,
As Death drew level, and head and head
    They swept t'ward the finish not far away.
Then he faintly smiled as the watchers bent
    To catch from his lips his last desire,
And he said, with a look of calm content,
" I 'm getting close to the judges' wire."

Who knows of this driver's death-bed dreams?
    Did he drive his races o'er again?
Did his thoughts go back to the thrilling scenes
    Of the track, from dying bed of pain?
Did he hear again the madd'ning cheers
    Of the crowd as he urged the gallant gray
To the wagon record that stood for years,
    And that stands by Time untouched to-day?

   .   .   .   .   .

They have laid him away in his last great sleep,
    In a narrow bed of the sexton's make,
But at the last, when the shadows creep,
    At the sound of the judges' bell he 'll wake,
And there we trust at the judges' stand
    He 'll be awarded a better place
Than ever even in thought he 'd planned,
    As he drove a horse in a waiting race.

BRIDE

OF MONTGOMERY.

I reckon you fellows know Bride — Ira E. Bride, of Montgomery.
Follered the horses for years, an' bin sellin' pools on the circuit;
Wears a plain suit o' blue jeans made down in Attakapas* Parish;
Cut on the bias an' gored, then tied like a sack in the middle.

---

* Pronounced Tuckapaw.

Queer sort o' fellow is Bride, jolly, rotund an' good-natured;
Fond o' his mint-juleps, too, an' a mighty fine judge o' good eatin';
Knows all the horsemen by sight, an' the horses 'way back to Gray
    Eagle;
Claims that his suit is hand-made by the fellow that one time
    owned Lightnin'.

English he is to the core, an' so, when the snows o' the winter
Fall to the bosom o' earth, wings he his way to the south'ard,
Down where the orange trees bloom, an' thar, 'neath the snowy
    magnolias,
Sips he mint-juleps again an' laughs at the winds o' December.

Takes he the world as it comes. Lets to-morrow take care of
    to-morrow;
Never bets nothin' himself on the races — that's nothin' to speak of;
Keeps his eyes open for jobs. If he sees 'em he doesn't say
    nothin',
Just pockets his little per cent. for holdin' the money o' others.

Fond he is, too, o' the girls, an' the glimpse o' a neatly turned
    ankle
Will bring the light into his eyes an' set his great heart
    a-jumpin',
'Till the sound o' its beats can be heard like the sound o' a
    mighty trip-hammer,
Wakin' the echoes at dawn when the iron hisses white on the
    anvil.

'Twas at Memphis one night in the fall, an', the pool-sellin' bein'
    all over,
Bride stood just outside the hotel, when there tugged at his elbow
    a stranger
Who had a sure thing for next day, the surest yet seen on the
    circuit —
A horse that could win in a walk, an' he wanted old Ira to play it.

Bride listened in peace to his tale, an' then, givin' a hitch to his
blue-jeans,
He pulled out his briar-wood pipe, an', fillin' it up with tobacco,
Scratched coolly a lucifer match in a calm, thoughtful way on his
breeches;
Then blew out a great cloud o' smoke an' told him he'd put
on the money.

Next day, when the sellin' began, Bride boomed the dark hoss
with his money,
Knocked down to himself every pool till he stood to win four or
five thousand;
Then stood with his glasses in hand, like Ajax defyin' the lightnin',
An' watched, in a manner intent, every jump that was made by
the hosses.

The dark hoss that Ira had backed on the word an' advice o' the
stranger
Led his field for two-thirds o' the route, an' then doubled up like
a jack-knife,
Stopped right at the head o' the stretch like he had been struck
by a cyclone,
An' faded away to the rear like a shadow that's lost in the sunlight.

Bride, cussin' himself for a fool, took a hack and drove back to
the city,
Belted 'round him his coat o' blue-jeans that was made down in
Attakapas Parish,
Drank a dozen mint-juleps or so, then started to hunt up the
stranger;
But the stranger had vanished an' gone, an' so had the money o'
Ira.

That's the reason that Bride doesn't bet, but leaves pickin' win-
ners to others;

Rests content with his little per cent. for holdin' the money o'
  strangers;
Takes sugar an' mint-leaves in his, an' sits with his eye on the
  crossin's,
Resplendent in suit o' blue-jeans made down in Attakapas Parish.

LITTLE SUNSHINE AND BONNIE GRACE.

'T was moah dan twenty yeahs ago.
  De white magnolia trees
War lookin' like great heaps ob snow,
  A-driftin' in de breeze;
De roses in de golden light
  War breakin' inter bloom;
De lilies in de sunshine bright
  Bent down to welcome June.

Dar came to de old Cap'ain's place,
  From far-off Nordern town,
A gal wif sunshine in her face
  An' har ob golden brown.
Her mouf were like a rosebud red,
  Half-hidden in de snow,
An' when she shook her curly head
  De sunbeams fell below

Her dimpled shouldahs, marble white,
  An' coiled upon her breas'
Like birds dat had grown tiahed ob flight
  An' foun' at las' deir nes'.
Her voice was like de golden bell
  Dat rings in heaben's street;
Her blue eyes seemed to cast a spell
  On all she chanced to meet.

She war mighty fon' ob horses,
  And would of'en come to me
Fo' to talk about de crosses
  In some famous pedigree;
But de hoss dat mos' she 'd fancy
  War a mare called Bonnie Grace,
By ole Rebel, out ob Nancy,
  An' de pride ob all de place.

Bonnie Grace, too, larned to lub her,
  An' one night de Cap'ain said,
As he sof'ly bent above her,
  Wid his hand upon her head:
" Little Sunshine, fo' de shadows
  Dat you banished from de place
When you came across de meadows,
  I will gib you Bonnie Grace."

June went driftin' down de riber,
  On de boat o' Fader Time.
Summah days don' las' fo'eber —
  Wintah waits jes' down the line.
As de mont's went troopin' aftah,
  An' den vanished, one by one,
Little Sunshine's ripplin' laughtah
  Still made music in de sun.

Den, at las', a shadow fallin
  Settled on de deah ole home,
An' de angels 'gan deir callin'
  Little Sunshine fo' to come.
Den she faded as the day-time
  Fades along de wes'ern sky,
As the violets do in May-time,
  When dey widder up an' die.

'Pears dat Bonnie Grace war missin'
   Little Sunshine mo' dan all;
She would stan' fo' hours an listen
   In de clover for her call.
Wait until de darkness roun' her
   Fell a black an' sable cloak —
Till I sen' a man to fin' her,
   Lock her up in walls ob oak.

" Foun' her dead, her head a-restin'
On po' Little Sunshine's grabe."

Def came in de mild September,
   Sen' dar by de King ob kings;
Pears to me I mos' remember
   Little Sunshine's taking wings.
Angels opened wide de po'tals
   Fo' to let deir sistah in,
Whar de feet ob de immo'tals
   Res' fo'eber free from sin.

She war buried by de riber
  Whar de tangled grasses grow,
Whar de white magnolias eber
  Blossom out in drif's ob snow.
Bonnie Grace dat night war missin',
  But de light dat mawnin' gabe
Foun' her dead, her head a-restin'
  On po' Little Sunshine's grabe.

LEXINGTON: A FRAGMENT.

I 've a picture, time-discolored, hanging on my chamber wall,
Taken from an old oil-painting that to memory will recall

Years from now the ancient legends of those races run of old,
When the winters were of silver and the summer-times of gold,

On a race-track in the southlands, where those flying feet once
    trod,
That has blossomed out in gravestones, that has rippled up in sod.

And a marble shaft uprisen casts its shadow o'er the land,
Where in summers long forgotten once there stood the judges'
    stand.

Where the cypress boughs are weeping as they bend above the
    dead,
And the roses bud and blossom, dust to dust again is wed.

And the cry of stricken mourners that is muffled up in tears
Sadly sweeps along the greensward that once echoed back the
    cheers

Of an eager crowd that, waiting, in the shadow and the sun,
Hailed the mighty son of Boston, the immortal Lexington.

'T is a picture of a stallion, standing where the robins call,
'Neath an ivy vine that clambers o'er a ruined garden wall.

And the tendrils overhanging almost fall upon his back,
And I fancy he is list'ning for the music of the track.

With his blaze face and white stockings, as he stands there in
　　the sun,
Looks he like some mighty monarch dreaming o'er his battles
　　won.

Blind, he peers about, but sees not.　Now and then he pricks his
　　ears,
List'ning for the judges' summons, waiting vainly for the cheers

That were wont of old to greet him when he trod the track a
　　king,
When men met and told each other of his greatness in the ring.

Lord and master of the harem, in his paddock all alone,
Sighs he for new worlds to conquer?　Dreams he of another
　　throne?

　　　　.　　　　　　.　　　　　　.　　　　　　.

O'er a little mound at Woodburn drifts in winter-time the snow,
And the blossoms fall upon it when the summer breezes blow.

There the hero blind is sleeping, but his mem'ry lives, to-day,
Ever in the hearts of turfmen, fresh as hawthorn buds in May.

Sire was he of horses fleeter than the Arab barbs of old
That were counted in the desert worth their weight in virgin gold.

Whispers fly about the race-tracks when some mighty deed is
　　done:
"'T is no more than we expected from the blood of Lexington!"

McCARTHY'S PLUG HAT.

(CHICAGO, 1887.)

Of all the queer sights that a mortal has seen
Since fairies first gamboled and played on the green,
And rode the black crickets about in their mirth,
When the night dropped its black velvet mantle to earth,
To the stage coach they drove in my grandfather's days,
That tumbled and lurched o'er the corduroy ways —
The strangest of all, seen in palace or flat,
Was worn by McCarthy, and called a plug hat.

" It looms up like a light-house seen through a fog."

The name of its maker the Lord only knows;
Its trials and troubles, its sorrows and woes,
Have so changed its appearance, McCarthy himself
Has forgotten its looks when it lay on the shelf.
It might have been white in some far-away day;
It might have been yellow, slate-colored or gray;
It might have been striped and streaked like a cat;
It's a queer combination — McCarthy's plug hat.

It looms up like a light-house seen through a fog;
It resembles a wart that has grown on a log.
If a knight of St. Patrick could borrow that tile
To wear on parade, how the lasses would smile.
The smoke and the dust that have rolled o'er its rim
Have left it discolored from crown down to brim.
It might have been purchased at Poverty Flat,
So out of all fashion 's McCarthy's plug hat.

Whenever McCarthy appears on the track,
He's a crowd of admirers that stand at his back.
In open-eyed wonder they look and they smile,
As they take in the shape of his queer-looking tile;
And even the steed that goes hurrying by
Gives a whinny of mirth as it catches his eye.
For nothing so strange, in palace or flat,
Has ever been seen as McCarthy's plug hat.

THE TOUT'S STORY.

Well, yes, you are right, sir — I am a tout —
    Been around among horses all my life,
And been kicked, sir, and cuffed, and knocked about
    Like a shuttlecock, in this world o' strife.

Have I made any money ? Yes, sir, some,
    And I made it, too, in an honest way.
It was out o' the books it had to come,
    Though they got the most o' it back next day.

No, I haven't got any now, you 're right;
    But then life is full o' these ups and downs:
For Dame Fortune will sweetly smile one night,
    Then perhaps the very next day she frowns.

I thought, sir, that Belle o' the West would win;
  She ran a good second the other day.
This time she was really the last horse in.
  It 's funny, sir, ain't it? But that 's their way.

Horses, you know, are most uncertain things—
  There 's no one can tell just what they will do;
Yet racing, they say, is " the sport o' kings,"
  And I think for that very reason too.

For only a king, so it seems to me,
  With the wealth of a kingdom at his back,
Can afford to plunge on the racers. See?
  They 'll cripple him then ere he leaves the track.

How do I fancy the life of a tout?
  Well, sometimes I like it, and sometimes not.
We float with the tide and we drift about,
  Till we settle down in a graveyard lot.

In summer the life is not hard at all.
  We can sleep out-doors in the tangled grass,
While the whip-poor-wills sweet all 'round us call,
  And the shadows o' night-time come and pass.

I 'll warrant you, sir, on the dew-wet ground,
  With a star-gemmed blanket over my head,
I can sleep as peacefully and as sound
  As can you at home in your downy bed.

But, sir, in the winter-time, when the snow
  Drifts high and eddies about in the street,
It 's hard on a chap with no place to go
  And half o' the time not enough to eat.

Then we see strange things in our travels, too.
  The owners fool us whenever they can.

Here 's a little yarn that I 'll spin to you,
    For they tell me you are a writing man.

It concerns the Derby, four years ago,
    That the folks all thought that Miss Ford would win.
I 'd been nosing 'round, and I thought somehow
    There were stable secrets I might get in.

For those chaps that came from the Golden State
    Had a string o' horses, and all well-bred.
That they 'd win the Derby as sure as fate
    Was the strange idea that entered my head.

What they could win with I didn't then know —
    They hadn't run anything up to that date.
They 've something good, sir, wherever they go,
    And I made up my mind to watch and wait.

At last I settled the thing in my mind
    That a chestnut colt was the one they 'd run,
And I tried to think of a way to find
    Out just how good was the work that he 'd done.

About his stable I managed to lurk
    From the early dawn till the sun had set,
But never a sign could I see of work,
    Save the long slow gallops the colt would get.

Then one night a thought crept into my mind:
    There 's no use getting up with the lark:
If it 's the public they 're trying to blind,
    They 'll send that chestnut along in the dark.

So that same night, sir, I made me a bed
    In the long, deep grass near the timer's stand,
And there, with the stars shining bright o'erhead,
    I was lulled to sleep by a cricket band.

It must have been about two in the morn
  That something woke me.   It might have been Fate.
I looked for a day that was yet unborn,
  And I heard the click o' the stable gate.

Then I saw some shadowy forms appear
  On the dusty track at the farther end
O' the stretch, and, crouching down in my fear,
  I watched them slow circle around the bend.

As nearer they came I could just make out
  A colt that was mostly hidden from sight
By a blanket, while they led him about,
  Making up their plans for a moonlight flight.

At each quarter pole they posted a man,
  With his lantern alight to wave in air,
When the colt that they tried on past him ran
  To signal the fact to the timers there.

Then the colt was galloped and well cooled out;
  The last instructions were given the jock,
To break away at a point on the route
  They had marked for him with a piece o' rock.

Next I heard the sound o' his flying feet
  As he broke away, and a swinging light
On the stable-turn, where the shadows meet,
  Told me that the chestnut was full in flight.

The mile was done, and still faster he flew.
  His rattling hoofs, like the sound of a drum,
Shook off from the blades o' the grass the dew
  And left them dry to burn up in the sun.

He finished flying, sir, right at the stand,
  And I, listening, heard an old man say:

" There 's not a race-horse in all the land
  That 's fitter than he for a Derby play."

They never knew, sir, not one o' the crowd,
  A tout lay listening there in the grass;
Else they would never have spoken so loud
  O' their future plans — but we 'll let that pass.

Sufficient to say that I learned the name
  O' the chestnut colt and the time he 'd made.
They 've written it now on the walls o' fame.
  A winner from memory ne'er will fade.

Then I hunted up a man that I knew,
  A regular hummer, sir, he for style,
Who would bet o' money enough for two,
  And I told him the tale o' that moonlight tri'l.

You remember well how the race turned out;
  How the chestnut colt, at "thirty to one,"
Just beat Miss Ford by a nose.   No doubt
  You were there yourself, sir, and saw the fun.

That night when my friend divided with me
  The amount that he 'd won on Todd that day,
I 'd three thousand dollars; so you can see
  It looked like things were a-coming my way.

Then I went to plunging on every race;
  That I could beat them I 'd never a doubt.
So I backed my favorites straight and place,
  And in just four days they had cleaned me out.

Since then I 've been living from hand to mouth;
  Many a time I 've gone hungry to bed,
And I 've slept out-doors in the sunny south
  'Neath a big blue blanket the Lord had spread.

What? How will it end? Well, God only knows.
In a nameless grave, though, like as not.
What difference, then, sir, whether it snows,
Or whether the sunbeams are burning hot?

You are going, are you? Ah, well, good night.
If there 's anything good I 'll come to you.
You look like a chap as would treat one right.
That tale about Todd and his trial is true.

BUDS OF SPRING.

Bold, blustering March, with bated breath,
Steals quickly through the woods away,
And with him go the chills of death,
That fade before the perfect day,

While, half in laughter, half in tears,
Comes April with its sun and showers —
A maiden full of hopes and fears,
Whose footsteps wake the sleeping flowers.

The maples bud and blow in leaves;
The bare brown fields are turned to green;
The wheat gives promise of the sheaves
That later in the year are seen.

The grand old broodmare looks with pride,
The while she hears the robins sing,
Down at the two foals at her side —
Her coming flyers — Buds of Spring.

" Her coming flyers—Buds of Spring."

II.
"RANK OUTSIDERS."

"RANK OUTSIDERS."

. ·.

THE OLD MAN AND THE FAST MAIL.

Young man, I am tired and weary, and I'll borrow your chair
    awhile,
To sit by your office window, where the golden sunbeams smile;
For I've driven from home since morning, although I am old and
    gray,
To see Uncle Sam's pet hobby, the Fast White Mail, to-day.

How time keeps a-ringing his changes!   It ain't many years ago
Since I traveled this same road, youngster, in a stage coach old
    and slow.
There wasn't a sign of a railroad, nor a telegraph pole in sight,
And the earth lay asleep in a mantle of snow-flakes pure and
    white.

A little log cabin, yonder, peeped out at the edge of the wood,
Like the face of a nut-brown maiden from under her snow-white
    hood,
And there we unhitched our horses, in the twilight cold and gray,
To rest from our weary journey till the dawn of another day.

I came here again the next summer, when meadows with grass
    were green,
When birds were at play in the oak trees, and fish asleep in
    the stream,
And I built, in a little clearing 'way yonder over the hill,
A cabin of logs and brushwood; and, stranger, I live there still.

But the cabin of logs has vanished.   There stands in its place
   to-day
A mansion of brick and granite, while over across the way
My lad has built him a cottage — a cottage he calls his own,
That discounts the big brick mansion where the old man isn't at
   home.

" They didn't think that the stage coach was lumberin', old and slow."

For old dogs don't learn new habits, and an old man's hard to
   please;
It 's not easy to rest from labor when one isn't used to ease.
Yet I don't know as I 'd be willin' to toil in the fields again,
A-workin' for paper dollars and a-killin' both heart and brain.

Once a week we got our mails then.   Folks wa' n't in a hurry to
   go.
They didn't think that the stage coach was lumberin', old and
   slow;
You couldn't have made us believe it, if you 'd argued an hour
   or more,
They 'd be carryin' mails by steam power an' throwin' em off at
   the door.

"And then, as away it vanished, with a flash like a comet's tail,
He said, 'Old Time, you're euchred by steam and a Fast White Mail.'"

Now cars run over their road-beds with the speed of a gust of
wind;
They 've left the lumberin' stage coach and the old-fashioned
ways behind,
And they tell me to lands far westward, where the eagle has left
its trail,
Uncle Sam is sendin' 'em letters by way of a Fast White Mail.

Well, times are a-changin' surely. One is never too old to learn,
Though there may be flaws in the marble my old eyes can't
discern;
Yet I 'm tired o' the deacon's croakin'. I wish he 'd give us a rest.
God 's runnin' this world, I reckon, and He doeth what seems the
best.

So I 've driven from home since mornin', although I am old and
gray,
To see Uncle Sam's pet hobby, the Fast White Mail, to-day.
In twenty-six hours, they tell me,—and it beats an old man like
me,—
They 're readin' the New York papers in the Queen of the Inland
Sea.

Now I 'll move my arm-chair, youngster, and sit where the bright
sun smiles,
Till I hear on the curve down yonder the whistle of old John
Miles;
For they tell me he runs an engine on the Fast White Mail
to-day,
And he runs like a reckless fellow if his hair *is* turnin' gray.

. . . .

The old man sat by the window till we saw o'er the curve below
The smoke from the coming engine like the wings of a great black
crow.
Then he crept with a gait unsteady out o'er the office floor,
And stood like a statue, watching the train from the open door.

It came like a great white arrow, tipped with a barb of steel,
Spurning the road beneath it with the touch of its iron-shod wheel;
Catching the mail while passing, with a demon's outstretched
    hand,
To be scattered in showers of blessings afar o'er a peaceful land.

Old Miles, with his hand on the lever, looked out as he passed
    the door,
Looked out at the sunbeams stealing swift clear down to the lake's
    green shore,
Then pulled the throttle wide open and seemed with his air to say,
" Uncle Sam, I could beat the lightning with your Fast White Mail
    to-day."

The old man looked in wonder as they caught the mail below.
" Aye, times are fast," he muttered, "for that idee ain't slow."
And then, as away it vanished, with a flash like a comet's tail,
He said, " Old Time, you 're euchred by steam and a Fast White
    Mail."

AN OUTCAST'S STORY.

(Told Beneath a Chandelier.)

Why tell you my story ?   What good will it do ?
The tale of an outcast won't interest you.
Well, if you insist, sir, my name here is Rose —
Of course, not my real name, as every one knows.
And I 'm just twenty-three, but was never a wife;
Yet since I was eighteen I 've followed this life.
God knows, if I could, I would leave it to-day.
Why don't I ?   Ah, sir, you don't know what you say.
But here ! draw your chair, sir, up closer to mine.
Yes, thank you, I will; for this generous wine
Serves to make me forget I once might have been
A proud, happy wife — not the plaything of men.

The die has been cast. 'T is too late to recall
The love and respect that I lost by my fall.
Remember this, sir: that a man was to blame
For my sin and sorrow — my fall and my shame.

In a little country village,
　　Where the apple-blossoms turn
Pink and white in early springtime,
　　And where the red sumachs burn
In the golden days of autumn,
　　Like to torch-lights on the wall,
Lived a simple country maiden,
　　Loved and petted, sir, by all.

Around the cottage where she lived
　　Climbed the roses, white and red,
And the birds among the maples
　　Laughed and chattered overhead.
Naught knew she of care and trouble;
　　Sang she gaily all day long,
While the robins seemed to listen
　　And to echo back her song.

Pride was she of all the village,
　　And her father, old and gray,
Loved her as he loved the sunshine
　　Drifting o'er his darkened way;
While her mother, old and feeble,
　　Fairly worshiped at her shrine,
Prayed that God would bless and keep her,
　　In that far-off happy time.

Grew the girl in grace and beauty,
　　As the years crept swiftly by.
To her cheek there crept the roses,
　　And the violets to her eye.

White and full the throbbing bosom
  That beneath her bodice lay;
Arms as round as ever sculptor
  Modeled fanciful in clay.

Suitors plenty came to woo her,
  But to none she gave her heart;
Dreamed she of a prince, who, coming.
  Of her life should be a part.
Once somewhere she 'd read the story
  Of a king who long ago
Wooed a beggar maid and won her.
  Might a prince not woo her so?

Came a young man to the village
  From the city far away —
Came to dream there in the sunshine,
  While the reapers made their hay.
Wooed with tender words the maiden,
  Wooed her as a prince might woo;
Hand in hand they walked together
  In the starlight and the dew.

Then one night, when all were sleeping
  In the village, 'neath the stars,
Stole the maiden forth to meet him
  By the lonely meadow bars,
Where a carriage stood in waiting.
  Not until the early dawn
Did the broken-hearted old folks
  Know their pet and pride had gone.

How I loved him none will know, sir —
  God help me, I love him still,
Though he robbed my life of sunshine —
  Though he worked me naught but ill.

Fled we to a distant city,
  Where at last my babe was born,—
Dead, for which I thanked the Savior,—
  For he left me that same morn.

Back to life I somehow drifted,
  Though I often prayed to die,
While there passed my life before me
  Like a shadow flitting by.
Work I sought, but none would give it:
  I had left the narrow lane
For the highway broad of pleasure,
  And it ended in my shame.

So one night, when weak and famished
  Bidden by the tempter's spell,
Entered I the stately portals
  Of King Pleasure's gilded hell.
Many men here join our revels,
  Stopping not to count the cost.
Leaving, still they 're social lions,
  But the woman, sir, is lost.

There, sir, is my story.   God pity the maid
Who falls as I fell, for the price that I paid
Was my peace on earth.   Oft I dream when alone
Of the roses that blossom about my old home.
I cry out to Death from the depths of despair;
I 'd pray if I thought Christ would answer my prayer.—
Excuse me, you come here for pleasure, and I—
I 'll try and laugh now, so you 'll think it a lie.

BILLY BROWN OF KOKOMO.

There lived down in Indiana, in a little country town,
Years ago, a slick young fellow that the boys called Billy Brown.
He was captain of a base ball team and good at any game,
But his skill at playing billiards was what gave him all his fame.

He had first begun to practice with the cue when quite a lad,
And his love of playing billiards often made the old man sad.
He soon caught the trick of nursing, and would lead them up the
    rail
As though they were but tiny ships being blown before the gale.

One by one the boys were beaten; one by one the men went down,
And in time the youngster blossomed out as champion of the
    town.
All the drummers learned to know him, and to know him to their
    cost.
Billy played them all for money, and the drummers always lost.

Then he practiced cushion caroms, learned the balk-line game
    to play,
And his head kept ever swelling, swelling, swelling, day by day.
Sighed he for new worlds to conquer, that should add unto his
    fame.
Trav'ling men no longer played him: they had tumbled to his
    game.

" Boys, I 'm going to Chicago," Billy said one night in fall,
" To the city by the lakeside, and I guess I 'll beat them all.
Schaefer may be quite a player, but I 've got my stroke, you see,
And he 'll think he 's struck a cyclone when he gets to playing
    me."

        .   .   .

'T was one cold night in November, when the streets were
    wrapped in gloom,
That a group of billiard players idly sat in Schaefer's room.

" Still from Schaefer's magic cue
One by one the points kept dropping, as at twilight drops the dew."

Swung the door upon its hinges, and there entered Billy Brown,
Laid a hundred on the table, with a challenge to the town.

Silence fell upon the players, as the night upon the deep,
For the stranger's nerve, like Carter's, nearly put them all to
sleep.
But, at last, a little German said, in accents halt and lame,
"Vell, I blays you for dot hundert, ef you blay der four-ball
game."

"I'm not playing now with infants," Billy answered with a smile,
Never dreaming 't was the Wizard he was talking to the while.
"Play two hundred points at balk-line for this hundred-dollar
bill."
Jacob scratched his head a moment; then he answered, "Vell,
I vill."

Shook the listeners' sides with laughter, as they gathered 'round
the pair,
Caught Brown's look of calm contentment and Jake's hesitating
air.
Soon the ivories were spotted, and the bank was won by Brown,
Who rolled thirteen points together, smiling blandly, and sat
down.

Jacob followed with a single, failing on a cushion shot.
Billy added ten to his string, and remarked that "Ten's a lot."
By a drive across the table Jacob got the balls in place;
Up and down the lines he drove them, leading them a merry race.

Swiftly clicked the balls together, and the buttons on Jake's string
Flocked together like to blackbirds that have tired upon the wing
And have settled down to rest awhile upon the slender wire
That girdles the wide world around and writes down thoughts in
fire.

Soon the marker called " One hundred ! "   Still from Schaefer's
    magic cue
One by one the points kept dropping, as at twilight drops the dew.
Massés, follows, spreads and forces, all were made with easy grace,
While a startled look of wonder chased the smiles from Billy's face.

Then the marker called " One-eighty," then " One-ninety-nine
    and game."
Jacob coolly took Brown's money — asked him would he call again.
" Who is that ? " gasped Brown, in wonder, and his mustache
    upward curled
As the answer came: " Jake Schaefer, champion player of the
    world."

    .   .   .   .

In a town in Indiana, known to fame as Kokomo,
Brown & Son are selling hardware in a little wooden row.
Billy keeps the books, and answers, when he 's asked to play a
    game:
" No; I once crossed cues with Schaefer, and I 'll never play again. "

THE NEW MAGDALEN.

The *Memphis Appeal*, some years ago, told the story of a fallen woman of that place, Mollie Cook by name, who, owning a gilded palace of sin, turned it into a hospital for the yellow-fever sufferers, and with her own hands nursed the sick and dying back to life again, until at last, wearied and exhausted with the long watching, she, too, fell a prey to the fever. I am told that a marble shaft, the gift of the city, marks her last resting-place in the cemetery there; and it seems but a fitting tribute to one who gave all she had — her life —to redeem the errors of the past.

The yellow death came stealing swift
　　Up from the river's edge —
Up from the dark, dank morasses,
　　With their tangled fringe of sedge;
Up from the misty black bayous,
　　On the south wind's tainted breath,
Till the skies grew dark at Memphis
　　With shadowy wings of death.

Then the air grew dense and silent,
　　And the wild bird ceased its song,
While strong men cried out in anguish,
　　"How long, O God! how long?"
But the skies gave back no answer.
　　Death's pitiless scythe still swung
As the reaper gathered his harvest —
　　A harvest of old and young.

The babe in its cradle sleeping,
　　In the flush of the morning light,
A smile on its dimpled features,
　　In a coffin slept at night;
While the man who knelt at even,
　　Thanking God for strength He gave,
Lay down to sleep at the dawning
　　In the cold and narrow grave.

The pavements only echoed back
    The wheels of the passing hearse
That bore to the silent city
    The victims of the curse —
The voices of stricken mourners,
    Who heard not the rustling wing,
But saw on the sleeper's forehead
    The seal of the Saffron King.

Then out from a gilded palace
    Of sorrow and sin and shame,
Clad in her robes of scarlet,
    A fallen woman came.
And songs of the noisy revel
    Gave place in its stately hall
To prayers for the sick and dying,
    And a woman's soft foot-fall.

And back from King Death's dark portals,
    From verge of an unseen land,
Came many a wandering mortal,
    At touch of that woman's hand;
Till the fever, wrathful, sullen,
    Touched her with its tainted breath,
And, asleep in a snowy garment,
    She lay in the arms of Death.
        .   .   .   .

O girl with the jeweled fingers!
    O maid with the laces rare!
Will that woman's grander action
    Count less than your studied prayer?
Have the angels, looking earthward,
    A love that's tenderer seen
Than that of this fallen woman,
    The true new Magdalen?

THE MODERN STYLE.

Do you remember, Tom, my boy, the old church on the hill ?
I used to go there when a lad, and I can see it still;
With ivy climbing o'er the roof and clustering round the door,
By which I used to wait for Sue in happy days of yore.
Ah, that was ere my hair turned gray, in days of long ago,
For Susie many years has slept beneath the winter's snow.

" The old church fell to ruins, Tom, beneath the touch of Time."

The old church fell to ruins, Tom, beneath the touch of Time,
Yet left somewhere within my heart a mem'ry half divine.
The preacher of the olden days has been for years at rest,
And violets blossom in the grass that grows above his breast.
The old-time choir of rosebud girls have drifted out of sight;
The leader with his tuning-fork has bid the world good-night.

They 've built a new church now in town upon a thoroughfare
That isn't like the old at all.   The other night, when there,
I couldn't help but sit and think about the olden ways
Of worship, when they feared the Lord and loved to sing His
        praise.
The ladies didn't go to see which was the latest style
Of bonnet, and to gossip of their neighbors all the while.

The new church, Tom, is built of stone, a monument to pride,
With steeple towering to the sky and portals open wide.
The sunbeams wander in by day through windows of stained
  glass,
Where shadows turn to clouds of gold, as swift they come and
  pass.
It costs a thousand dollars, Tom, to rent a pew per year !
A privilege to worship God is sold now mighty dear.

The preacher wears a broadcloth coat, and in a quiet way
He talks about the Lord as though he met Him every day;
He never mentions hell at all — 't would make the people smile —
For hell is something, Tom, that's gone completely out of style.
It wouldn't do to tell a man who gambles on the Board
His business was not quite the thing and might offend the Lord;
And if you barred the grab-bag out and left it in the lurch
You'd cut off half the revenue that helped to build the church.

The benches now are cushioned, Tom, so one can pray at ease,
For most of folks pray better when it does not hurt their knees.
You can't expect a business man to kneel upon hard oak,
And beg the Lord for something when he isn't really "broke."
He simply makes a calm request that God will see him through,
And give him frosted cake for one, instead of bread for two.

Folks go to church these latter days because it gives them tone,
Leave their religion at the door and never take it home,
Save in rare instances, perhaps — so rare these latter days
That those with true religion, Tom, hide it from public gaze:
They sit in their arm-chairs at home, and read God's holy word,
Kneel in their closets privately and worship there the Lord.

The world grows better day by day, I'm satisfied of that.
It's hard to be a Christian, though, and rent a modern flat.
It's hard to have to go to church and wear a tattered coat,
To hire a pew, way in the rear, and never hear a note

Of that sweet singer who is paid a gold-piece for each song —
To worship God by proxy when you really think it's wrong.

SANDY'S NUGGET.

(CALIFORNIA, 1852.)

Now, jest wait for awhile,
Jim; step up here an' smile:
I'm the happiest man in the mountains to-day,
An' I says it's my treat.
Will ye have straight or sweet?
Aye, that's right. Take yer bitters the regular way.

For them toddies an' such
To my taste aren't much.
Why, it's sp'ilin' good liquor to mix 'em that way.
Well, here's to you, old pard;
May you hold a trump card
In the great game of life, I'm a-wishing to-day.

Have I struck it? I guess
That I have, old boy. Yes,
And far richer than ever 't was struck here afore;
It's the first that's been found
In these mines. Weighs twelve pound.
Oh! Where is it? Up-stairs over Mattingly's store.

Is it pure? Yes, and sweet
As that rose at your feet,
For how could it get soiled on its journey to earth,
When the angels looked out,
Keeping guard on the route,
Till it came to our cabin with sunshine and mirth?

As to value, it's hard
To assess it yet, pard,
For it ain't been assayed 'cept by me an' my wife;
But this 'ere camp don't hold
Enough silver or gold
For to buy it.   On that you can wager your life.

Pretty steep, did you say ?
I don't think so, but — eh ?
Now, who said it was metal ?   I didn't — not I;
It 's a baby, with eyes
Just as blue as the skies,
An' a look like its mother's, so modest an' shy.

What ! A gal ? Yes, you bet,
She 'll be somethin' to pet
For the boys when she gets so she 's runnin' around.
Fill your glass up again;
I 'm the first to begin
On a family — an' here 's to the nugget I 've found.

II.

Now, the news of Sandy's fortune was soon spread about the camp,
    And the boys, they talked it over that same night at Haley's store,
And they called it " Sandy's Nugget," and thought him a lucky scamp,
    While they hoped he 'd be the father of a half-a-dozen more.

Then old Jim he said he reckoned, as it was the first to come,
    That it ought to have a send-off, and to this the boys agreed;
So they called a sort of meeting for to see what should be done,
    To get up a celebration such as never yet was seed.

Of the diff'rent things suggested thar I haven't time to speak,
    Until Jim proposed together they should call upon the kid
In their " Sunday-go-to-meetings," as the wise men went to seek
    Once the Christ-child in the Bible, and should do as those had did.

When they entered Sandy's cabin, Night had just let fall her bars,
  And the rough men kissed the baby, and beside it on the bed
Each one laid a bag of gold dust, while the mother's eyes, like stars,
  Grew so misty with the rain-drops that she turned away her
    head.

Old Jim came last, and, bending down, he kissed the baby girl,
  And beside her placed a package that was larger than the rest,
As he said, " Thar, Sandy's Nugget, ye shall be the miners' pearl,
  An' I 'll give ye most o' any, fer I loved yer mother best."

'T was full twenty thousand dollars that the miners left that night,
  And 't was all for Sandy's Nugget, as the boys had named the
    child.
" Fer," said Jim, " we 'll make her future, if we can, look gay an'
    bright. "
  And the richest girl at Haley's Bar looked up at him and smiled.

ME AND JIM.

We were both brought up in a country town,
    Was me an' Jim,
An' the hull world somehow seemed ter frown
    On me an' him.
At school we never was given a chance
To l'arn that Africa wasn't in France.
Patches we wore on the seats o' our pants,
    Did me an' Jim.

But we grew up hearty, an' hale, an' strong,
    Did me an' Jim;
We knowed ev'ry note in a thrush's song,
    Did me an' him;

An' we knowed whar the bluebirds built their nests
When the spring tripped over the mountains' crests,
Why the robins all wore their scarlet vests,
   Did me an' Jim.

Then we fell in love, jest as most folks do,
   Did me an' Jim;
We was arter the same gal, though, we two,
   That 's me an' him.
An' she treated us jest alike, did she,
When at quiltin'-party or huskin'-bee.
We was even up in the race, you see,
   Was me an' Jim.

I popped at last, an' she answered me " No."
   Jim followed suit,
But she wouldn't have him, an' told him so.
   Forbidden fruit
We called her then, an' I 'm rather afraid
That we cussed a little; an' then we prayed
That she 'd live an' she 'd die a plain old maid,.
   Did me an' Jim.

Then the war broke out, and Company B
   Caught me an' Jim.
We both on us fit fer the Union — see?—
   Did me an' him;
An' we heerd the screechin' o' shot an' shell,
The snarlin' o' drums, an' the rebel yell;
An' follered the flag through the battles' hell,
   Did me an' Jim.

'Twas the day that we fit at Seven Oaks,
   Death came to Jim,
An' excuse me, please. but I sorter chokes
   Talkin' o' him.

" And we knowed whar the bluebirds built their nests
When the spring tripped over the mountains' crests."

Me and Jim.

Fer his rugged brown hand I held in mine
Till his soul passed out through the picket line,
Whar an angel waited the countersign
   To git from Jim.

Then I fit along till the war was done,
   Without poor jim;
Was given a sword instead of a gun,
   An' thought o' him.
An' I wore an eagle, when mustered out,
On my shoulder-straps, an' I faced about
Fer the startin'-p'int o' my hull life's route,—
   But not wi' Jim.

I was quite a man in that country place
   I'd left wi' Jim.
She gave me a smile with a blushin' face,
   An' asked 'bout him.
So I told her how, as she sat 'longside,
Like a soldier brave he had fought an' died,
An' then—well, I kissed her because she cried—
   Kissed her fer Jim.

Then I married her one bright day in June,—
   Fer me an' Jim.
Oft under the light o' the stars an' moon
   We talked o' him.
An' arter awhile, when a baby came—
A boy—an' we looked for a proper name,
His memory comin' up fresh agin,
   We called him Jim.

HER EVENING PRAYER.

When the day burns out in crimson
　All along the western sky;
When Night's picket-line of shadows
　Draw with stealthy footsteps nigh.
Steals there softly to my chamber
　Little lass with eyes of blue,
And a sweet voice softly whispers,
　"Can't I say my prayers to you?"

Then she straightway kneels before me,
　Clasps her dainty hands in prayer,
While the firelight's crimson glory
　Turns to burnished gold her hair.
"Kiss me first," she softly whispers,
　"Den I'll say dem awful dood."
And two roguish eyes peer at me
　From beneath her tangled hood.

Tenderly I bend to kiss her,
　Press my lips on eyes and hair.
"Now," she says, "Papa, I'm yeddy,
　You must listen to my prayer."
From a heart that knows no malice,
　Upward float the simple words,
To the dear Christ-child who watches
　O'er His children and the birds.

Listen to her childish whisper —
　"Gentle Jesus, meek and mild."
Soft and low the sweet petition —
　"Look upon a little child."
Sinks her voice into a murmur —
　"Pity my simplicity."
Angels scarce can hear the prayerful
　"Suffer me to come to Thee."

"Oh, fain would I be brought to Thee,
    Dracious Lord; forbid it not."
Falls the golden head still lower
    Of my sleepy little tot.
Eye-lids now are growing heavy.
    "In the kingdom of Thy drace,"—
Hear, O Christ, the faintly whispered
    "Div a little child a place."

"Amen" follows, uttered quickly,
    As she starts up wide-awake,
Wraps her snowy robes about her,
    Gives her saucy head a shake.
"Didn't say dem all," she whispers,
    "Taus my eyes tept shuttin' tight.
Played too hard; besides, I'm finkin
    Maybe Dod is tired to-night."

MY FATHER'S MILL..

Ah, how well I remember the old brown mill
    That never was quiet the whole day long,
For the noisy hopper would never keep still,
    And the wheels forever were humming a song
As they answered the poor man's whispered prayer
    That he breathed each night by his lowly bed,
While the dust hung thick in the troubled air —
    "We are grinding for God thy daily bread."

Oh, the old mill's loft was a haunted place,
    And the dust lay thick on the rough board floor,
While over the rafters the rats would race
    As I laid my hand on its shrunken door,

Hurrying, scurrying, scampering by —
   Then peering out from their holes at me,
With a friendly nod and a laughing eye
   That said, " We are stealing the corn, you see. "

But the miller, who stood with his dusty coat,
   Whistling low, in the old mill-door,
And setting the ghost of a song afloat
   On the air, has crossed to the other shore,
Carrying with him the dreams he dreamed
   As the yellow meal, like a cloud, unrolled
From the wooden spout in the wall, and streamed
   To the floor beneath in a shower of gold.

Now a stranger stands in the miller's place,
   With a coat as white as the one he wore,
And two black eyes, from a round, red face,
   Peer out at me from the open door;
And I hear the hum of the whirling wheels,
   That turn the stones with a giant's power,
And I see the dust as it noiseless steals
   Through the old brown mill, like the ghost of flour.

Ah me! how the years have marched along,
   Since I tied the bags in that dingy place,
Where the wheels kept time to the miller's song
   And the buckets laughed in their upward race.
But still I hear in my dreams, to-day,
   The sound of the hopper, never still,
And I fancy I see the rats at play
   In the haunted loft of my father's mill.

" *The girls snuggled in,
with the boys at their
side.*"

THE OLD-FASHIONED WAY.

Oh, give me a ride in the old-fashioned sleigh
   With the old-fashioned girls that I knew in my youth,
Whose hearts were as light as the snow of to-day
   And whose eyes held a promise of sunshine and truth.

And give me the horses we bred on the farm,
   With their steady, slow ways as they traveled the road,
And give me the laughter and cries of alarm
   That came from the girls in the overturned load.

'T was a plain wagon-box that was half filled with straw,
   That the girls snuggled in, with the boys at their side,
And the buffalo robes, by an unwritten law,
   Were compelled to conceal what they sheltered with pride.

Then a sly kiss was stolen sometimes for a lark,
   When the shadows lay heavy and thick on the way.
" 'T was the driver's whip only that cracked in the dark,"
   We explained, and the lassies ne'er gave it away.

Oh, the buffalo robes were ne'er heavy enough,
   And the lassies, God bless 'em, they had to keep warm;
So waists were encircled with warm woolen stuff
   That hid in its linings a masculine arm.

Then just before dawn, at the night's darkest time,
　　When the lassies were left at the low cottage gate,
Came the whispered good-night from lips redder than wine,
　　And a kiss that was granted because it was late.

THE SENTINEL'S STORY.

We were standing on picket, he and I,
Out under the stars of a midnight sky,
In the Wilderness, where the night bird's song
Gives back an echo the whole night long;
Where the silver stars, as they come and pass,
Leave their stars of dew on the tangled grass;
Where the rivers sing in the darkest hours
Their sweetest songs to the listening flowers.

He 'd a slender form and a girlish face,
That I thought in the army out of place;
Though he smiled when I told him so one day —
Aye, smiled and blushed in a girlish way
That minded me of a face I knew,
In a Northern village 'neath the blue.
When the army marched by the meadow bars
She 'd kissed me, watched by the laughing stars.

Right before us the river silent ran.
　　We two had been placed there to guard the ford,—
A dangerous place,—and we 'd jump and start
　　Each time that a leaf by the wind was stirred.
Behind us the army lay encamped;
　　Their camp-fires burned into the night
Like bonfires built upon the hills,
　　And set by demon hands alight.

Somehow, whenever I looked his way,
  I seemed to see her face again,
Kind o' hazy-like, as you 've seen a star
  A-peepin' out through a misty rain;

"'Twas just in the flush of the morning light,—
We 'd stopped for a chat at the end of our beat."

And once, I believe, as I thought of her,
  I thought aloud, and I called him Bess,
When he started quick, and smiling said,
  "You dream of some one at home, I guess."

'T was just in the flush of the morning light —
    We 'd stopped for a chat at the end of our beat —
When a rifle flashed at the river's bank,
    And, bathed in blood, he sank at my feet.
All of a sudden I knew *her* then,
    And kneeling I kissed the girlish face,
And raised her head from the tangled grass
    To find on my breast a resting-place.

When the corporal came to change the guard
    At six in the morning, he found me there,
With Bessie's dead form clasped in my arms,
    And hid in my heart her dying prayer.
We buried her under the moaning pines,
    And never a man in the army knew
That dead Will Searles and my girl were one.
    You 're the first I 've told — the story is true.

MERCY MAY.

We were lovers, Mercy May and I,
    In the summers long ago,
When life was bright with love's young dream
And lily bells beside the stream
    Swung softly to and fro;
Ere came November's chilling winds.
    And fell the winter's snow.

She was all the world to me, and I
    Dream of her still to-day,
As of a sunbeam, warm and bright,
That lightened up life's stormy night,
    A rainbow in the spray;
Or as a vision vanishing
    Thro' heaven's gates away.

She sang.   The meadow-lark that sprang
   From out the grass was still.
Clear as a flute that sweet voice rang
   O'er valley, wood and hill.
And where she walked the violets grew
And opened wide their eyes of blue,
Tear-dimmed, and misty with the dew
   That stars at even spill.

'T was in the golden days of June
   I said to Mercy May,
The while we stood beside the sea:
"I love you; come and walk with me
   To lighten life's dark way."
She bent her golden head and blushed,
   But did not answer nay.

The summer sunbeams came and went;
   The wheat-fields turned to gold;
The nights grew longer, one by one,
And shadows lengthened in the sun
   As summer's days grew old;
The roses, blushing, bloomed and died —
   Were earth in earthy mold.

As die the roses, so she died
    One golden autumn day.
The angel with the rustling wings,
Before whose touch earth's proudest kings
    Become as common clay,
Touched her with fingers icy cold,
    And beckoned her away.

Now I alone am left to weep,
    To listen and to wait
The coming of the boatman pale
To row me through the misty veil,
    And open wide the gate
Where Mercy May will welcome me.—
    She promised she would wait.

Turned Out.

www.ingramcontent.com/pod-product-compliance
Lightning Source LLC
Chambersburg PA
CBHW021108020726
47500CB00003B/664